KEURIUM

A novel by

JS LEE

Pent-Up Press
ISBN-13: 978-1-7320943-2-1

그리움
KEURIUM

A longing for anything that has left a deep impression
in the heart—such as a memory, person, or place.

For Mia Lowe—
and the broken pieces within us
begging for truth, validation, and love.

ENTRANCE

I can't move, see, or speak.

Something snaps on my face. It's a mask. It feels plastic. They think it will save my life. It just makes it harder to breathe.

Push and pull. Poke and prod.

People are frantic. They speak all at once in a language I don't understand.

A needle stabs my arm.

The world… slows… down.

I might've entered a tunnel in the sky. The engine goes quiet.

From under my lids, I sense a change—in light, maybe. I'm rolled somewhere new.

Beep.

Beep.

Beep.

I hear someone speaking: "As far as we can tell, she's in there. Her EEG and neurological exams rule out a coma."

How I got here, no one knows.

OFF-WHITE CANVAS

Out of the white fog, a voice came through. It was Mother.

"I loved you the moment I saw your picture. It was a black and white mugshot. You were bald and kind of looked like an old Chinaman." She laughed. "But I knew that I loved you from the second I saw it. I felt it in here." She tapped her chest twice. "My only regret is that you weren't born from me."

As a toddler, I'd gaze up at the miraculous beauty of my mother without understanding I came from another. I felt her love back then when I was nothing but hope—a blank canvas waiting to be filled.

"You were meant to be ours." She stroked my hair and adjusted my dress as if I were one of her prized dolls. "You're going to add so much to this family. Someone up there in the sky had big plans for us all when they brought us together."

I was special as long as I was hers. And when I was undoubtedly hers, I hadn't a care in the world.

I was a rescue, you see.

Mother knew of this family who flew an Asian baby over to live with them. Everywhere they went, people would stop to ask questions, and her mother would proudly recite the heartwarming story. Soon enough, the same would be happening to us.

Despite already having two kids of their own flesh and

blood—Ivan and Myra, before Jack came along to make it three—our father wasn't one to turn her down. They waited two years for a match. And then within seventeen hours, I went from "a nobody with nothing to a somebody with everything," as she liked to say, adding, "But we're the lucky ones."

Everyone knew that last bit was a lie.

We lived in a mansion of a house on a ritzy cul-de-sac. My own private room was bright and bursting with floral patterns and lace. I had a double-wide closet filled with the latest clothes. My shelves were lined with one of Mother's doll collections. I'd come a long way from the overcrowded orphanage in Korea. I wouldn't dare deny it.

But, love? I couldn't wrap my head around it.

When I asked Mother if she loved me, she'd send me for a slow spin in the center of my room. There, I'd find proof of her love. Or, she'd start again with, "I loved you the moment I saw your picture." But the lack of a clear answer in present tense always left me hanging and kept me earning.

They say not to dwell on the negatives in life; that reality is mind over matter. Since my mind is all I seemingly have left, I try to steer it towards land. My oasis is this memory of Mother:

Elvis was crooning through the intercom system. I thought the house was shaking from the overloaded speakers, before realizing it was just me.

I was kneeling on the kitchen floor. I felt the prickly heat in my stout toddler legs as I carefully peered around the doorframe.

Mother was in a good mood. She held a can of pine-scented Pledge in one hand and a pink terry cloth rag in the other. Her bare feet swept side to side. She narrowed her sapphire eyes and puffed out her chest, clutching the can to her lips as she sang, "For my darlin', I love you… and I always will…"

The sunlight reaching in through the large picture window set her red hair on fire. She shined like a movie star. Her intricate blue silken housedress swung wide. She wore it several times a week before getting done up for the day. "It's Oriental," she liked to tell me, sweeping fingers across gold embroidery. When she wore it, I felt we were somehow the same.

My sister crouched down beside me. She whispered, "She's beautiful—isn't she, Shay?" tapping a hand to my thigh.

Nodding, we watched on in a trance. These magical moments of Mother's were rare. We knew to cherish each one, mesmerized and transformed.

Mother sang on. "For my darlin', I love you… and I always will…"

This is how I like to imagine her now. Every coin has two sides and if I had my way, Mother's would always land heads up.

It's been a few months since I've seen her. It's been days since I've seen anyone. But I hear them. They just don't know it.

GOD AND PERVERTS

"If you control your mind, you'll control your life," Mother said.

But now, with such limited control, it all comes flooding back—all the things I tried to forget.

In here, people see me but I can't see them. They touch me and I can't respond. And it's not the first time I've felt like this.

I used to have the ugliest dreams. Someone was watching me as I slept. I kept my eyes shut and ignored the monster at the foot of my bed, willing him away.

I'm not scared of you.

I'd lie still with my breath shallow. The ticking of the clock down the hall filled my ear drums with dread.

I thought, Maybe if I focused hard enough, I could disappear and the monster would, too.

Myra also had nightmares. She wouldn't talk about them, but I'd hear her groaning from down the hall. Sometimes she'd kick and shout. It felt strangely comforting to know we had something in common, even if it wasn't through blood. When I'd ask about it the next day, she'd look at me as if I were crazy. She's five years older, so I figure she was embarrassed for having them.

Even during the daytime, I often had the distinct feeling of being watched. My brother Ivan said I was paranoid. But you know that feeling you get when your skin crawls and you can't place why? I had that all the time.

When I got up the courage to ask Mother, she explained: "That's God. He's always watching. So you better be good—even when you don't think anyone is looking."

"How many Gods are there?"

"Just one, but he's got eyes everywhere that report back to him and everything gets filed into one big log."

I took a risk. "Are you God?"

Mother chuckled and shook her head. "Just make sure you do everything Mommy and Daddy say and you'll be fine."

I skipped out to the yard, where Myra was lounging in the grass in a fuchsia bikini that cast a pinkish glow on her skin. I asked, "Are you tired?"

"No," she huffed, examining her nails. "I'm getting some color."

"What for?"

"Because everyone looks better with a tan. Even Daddy says so."

I took off my dress and plopped down on the grass alongside her.

"What are you doing? Put your clothes on! There are perverts out there!"

I looked around and asked, "Where?" before climbing back into my dress.

"Everywhere. You just can't always see them."

And so I figured that explained the reason I always felt someone watching. "Is God a pervert?"

Myra howled with laughter. "I don't know," she considered, while filing her nails. "Maybe he is."

I flopped to my stomach, sifting through grass for daisies.

It was before I dubbed insects enemies, or felt the sting of my sister's disapproval. After twisting the fuzzy yellow center on my cheeks the way Myra put powder on hers, I plucked at the petals one by one.

"She loves me, she loves me not," I recited, with every two petals discarded.

"It's supposed to be 'he'," scoffed Myra—but I paid no mind.

When I got down to my last petal, I gasped. "She loves me!"

"Who loves you, you dyke?"

"Mommy!" I cheered, rolling onto my back.

Myra sheltered her face from the sun. She glared, rolled her eyes, and closed them again.

Smiling up at the clouds in the sky, it felt as if I had won the serendipitous love of my mother. But it was only a matter of time before I started messing up, chipping away at it.

COLORING OUTSIDE THE LINES

Not to brag, but I was known as the best colorer in kindergarten. I had a foolproof process. I traced the outlines with hard pressure and filled them in gently. All of my papers were pinned to the classroom walls and embellished with stars.

My first big offense started innocently enough.

The girl across from me was holding her crayon the way Mother stirred sauce in the pan. She looked like she was having the time of her life as she scribbled outside the lines without a care in the world. I wanted to know how that felt.

I picked up a yellow-orange Crayola and held it as if I were stirring the sauce. I bore down hard. It was like the page was a Ouija board and my hand a mere vehicle for the spirits. I picked up another color and carried on making the most delightful mess of my life. I lost myself completely. The regulator snapped off the engine. At last, I was free to see what my motor was made of.

The teacher crept up behind me, took the page from the table, and led me aside. Stern-faced but gentle-voiced, she asked, "What happened here?"

Clenching my muscles to keep my body from shaking, I employed my most natural shrug. I still buzzed from the joy ride. In a segment of my brain, I was still on it. But always eager to please the authorities, my stomach turned. For the first time, I was in trouble.

"You can do better than this. Don't you think?"

Embarrassed, I shrugged again.

I watched as she scribbled a note on the top right corner of my masterpiece. I could tell that, like most adults, she thought she was doing the right thing. But the thing about most adults is that they assumed because they were once your age, they knew what you needed.

"I want you to take this home for your mother to sign, okay?"

I nodded and returned to the table, hanging my head and kicking the floor. I resumed my old style of coloring so I could have something pretty to take home to soften the blow of the other.

When I hopped off the yellow bus that afternoon, Mother waited on the front steps of our giant house. She waved to the driver who, like every straight man, had somewhat of a thing for her. "Afternoon, Mrs. Stone!" he called.

"Hi, Harry," she cooed. "Thanks for my Chinese delivery!"

My jaw dropped.

Harry chortled. "My pleasure! Have a good day!"

Mother always said to correct people if they called me Chinese. She said they didn't know any better.

Mother knew better. She specified South Korean a dozen times a week to curious strangers.

I didn't have the words or the strength to address it. So I held out my coloring pages to get on with the rest of my shame.

Mother looked at the first page, nodded, and smiled. But as she flipped to the next, her face plummeted. "What's this? Why did you do this?" Her voice was more angry than unsure.

I didn't know how to explain that I just wanted to see what it felt like to do something different—to feel less controlled.

"This is terrible! If you know how to make pictures like this," she held up the tried and true, "then what on earth provoked this atrocity? You should be ashamed of yourself!"

She shoved me inside. I retreated a few layers deep into my shell.

Startled by the sudden slam of the front door, I offered a meager, "Sorry."

"You bet you are!" she spat. "Don't you think I do enough for you? Living's not free, you know. You're lucky to have food, clothes, and a roof over your head. The least you could do is make me proud of your God-given talents!"

I could feel her hot breath across my face as she towered above me. Her words lost all meaning as I tucked myself behind my brave facade. Her body shifted. "What have you got to say for yourself?" she hollered. "Answer me, young lady!"

I raised my head an inch but kept my focus on the white marble floor in between us. "I'm sorry. I won't do it again."

"You'd better not! Now get upstairs and go to your room. Don't come out till I call you. Scram!"

I walked into my room like it was a foreign country, not knowing where to go or what to do. I felt like a stranger in my own skin.

Sitting on my bed with a straight back and hands folded, I vowed to never disappoint Mother again. But some promises are hard to keep no matter how hard you try.

NOT MOTHER

I inhale the soft scent of vanilla. It's Jae-Mee. His hair product gives him away as he enters the hospital room.

I roll the vanilla around on my tongue as it lights up the vibrant map of our old life in my brain. Late Sunday mornings in bed. The quick shiver of water that misses your mouth when it drops onto your slumberous skin. The cat's sweeping tail sticking fur to your unwashed face as you wrangle the covers for two more sacred minutes.

I imagine my finger floating through the air as I paint the way his jet black hair trickles down the sharp curve of his cheekbones. I want to turn my head, pop open my eyes and let them devour him whole.

"Hey." He pauses. "I'd say happy birthday, but it's obviously not one."

Right. Today I turn thirty-seven—so they say.

The chair squeaks as he settles into it. "Miss you. Paisley does, too. They been treating you alright? Listen to me—like you can answer."

The heel of his foot tap tap taps the floor. He has a habit of bouncing his knee when nervous.

"So, catatonia... I Googled it about fifty times but don't really get it. I keep wondering, what'd I miss?"

The air in the room feels constrained—like we've just had

a fight.

Jae-Mee's quiet. "Fuuuuuck," he whispers.

What I'd give to reach out my arm, rub his back, and tell him it's okay. It's going to be fine. But I can't. And I don't know if that's true.

"I can't seem to get ahold of your mother. Myra says she's too upset to talk but... whatever."

Mother. I nearly forgot about her for a minute. She must be spreading her avoidance of me onto Jae-Mee.

"I called your boss. He said to say they're all rootin' for ya."

He carries on but I'm tuned out, still thinking of Mother. I wonder if she's been thinking of our last altercation. Does she have any regrets, like I do? Or maybe regrets—like: me?

Or maybe Mother's ignoring Jae-Mee because the truth is, she never really liked him. She'd comment that he wasn't driven enough, but I know she'd prefer me with a white man—someone more like them than me.

For the first thirty-odd years, I felt the same way. I had no interest in Asian men. Being with one would only make me appear more Asian. And I didn't feel Asian inside, so appearing more Asian would come with even more expectations that I couldn't live up to. I wanted camouflage. And I was dumb enough to believe the more white people I shoved in front of me, the better I'd blend. Of course, all it did was make me stand out even more.

Besides, there were no Asian men in the white world that I lived in. And the few I encountered on the periphery weren't interested in this whitewashed wreckage. I had no sense of culture or traceable bloodlines for their parents' approval.

And then I met Jae-Mee.

Oh shit.

He sighs. "Well, that's all I can think of. Maybe next time I'll bring something to read so I don't babble on like an idiot."

Guilt washes over me for getting carried away in my head during the short time we had. The lack of eye contact makes it harder to focus. It's too easy to chase butterflies downstream.

When he leans down to kiss my forehead, soft fabric brushes across my chin—and I know that he's wearing that bright aqua sweater I love, that makes his dark features pop. Not being able to appreciate him as much as he deserves is cruel to us both.

"Don't forget to make a wish."

As he pulls himself away, I can't help but wonder how I can be so lucky and unlucky at once.

IF YOU DON'T, I WILL

As I hear Mother's threat echo through my head, I shove it away like a fib from an unsavory source. Maybe the drugs they've got pumping through me is some sort of truth serum. It reminds me of that scene from "A Clockwork Orange" where the protagonist's eyes are peeled open and forced to watch.

I see the closed bathroom door and hear water running. And then I'm dropped in.

Although Mother's a natural redhead, she intensifies it with Clairol. Before I learned that, all I knew was that she locked herself in the bathroom and I wanted to be where she was. I enjoyed my time alone, but kids are like cats—beyond the shut door is the place to be.

I knocked carefully.

"Leave me alone!" Mother bellowed.

I jumped back from the door and bumped into Myra, who was snickering and leaning against the blank wall. Mother never bothered decorating the miles of wall space in the hallways. No frames, no wallpaper, no mirrors.

Myra shook her head. "She'll never let you in."

"How come?"

"Because she's killing herself."

She said it with a straight face, and while I didn't

necessarily believe her, I banged on the door again.

"Do you hear the water running? That's so you don't hear her scream."

In my young mind, her reasoning made sense. I started pounding and kicking the door in, desperate to keep Mother alive. Myra watched, unfazed.

The door finally flung open and Mother appeared. She looked like an alien potato left in the cupboard, with a plastic bag over her head and pieces of hair sprouting through it. I hardly recognized her face, it was so contorted.

And then it came.

"If you don't leave me alone right now, I'm going to kill myself!" she screamed, slamming the door in my face.

I was shocked and horrified.

I peered at Myra, who laughed. "See? Told you." She skipped off down the hall.

I followed her out to the yard. She sat with her back against the crabapple tree, holding a mirror between her knees. Chomping on winterfresh gum, she turned her head this way and that, brushing her hair to the side with her fingers.

I sat on the grass a few feet away and crossed my legs. "Why does Mommy want to kill herself?"

"She doesn't, stupid." Myra's eyes didn't leave her reflection. She smiled at herself, batting her lashes playfully.

"Then why'd she say it?"

"So we'd do what she wanted."

"Then why'd you say she was going to before?"

"I was teasing," huffed Myra. "Can't you take a joke?"

I felt dumb when I didn't get something, so I kept quiet. Squinting up at the maroon-purple leaves, I plucked fistfuls of grass and threw them into the wind.

"Quit it," groaned Myra, flipping through a magazine.

"Why doesn't Mommy go to our hairdresser?"

"She does. But she dyes it at home."

"Why?"

"Oh my God, you ask way too many questions. Why do you think? She doesn't want anyone to know she colors it."

I watched Myra twist her beautiful red hair—just like Mother's—into a side-braid. I glanced down at my own boring hair and thought of something a teacher had told me— that we can be anything we want in life. Leaning back, breathing in the freshly cut grass, I envisioned a whole new me. If I could be pretty like Myra and Mother, I was certain everything else would be great.

"Do you think she could color mine, too?"

Myra dropped her mirror. Her head tilted towards the branches as she cackled, nearly knocking herself out on the tree. She heaved forward, headbutting the ground. When she finally caught her breath, she said, "Oh my God. That would look so stupid!"

I jumped as a crabapple fell, barely missing my head. That set her off again. And so I laughed along with her because, in my mind, that's what sisters were supposed to do.

Something shifts me back to the present. I still hear Myra's laughter, along with other times Mother threatened us with her death, overlapping in rounds in my head.

A few years ago, when I asked her about it, Myra said, "She never said that. You're crazy."

I wonder how she could forget such a thing. And I wonder how I could make it all up.

THE JELL-O CAKE

Humor was not one of Mother's qualities. Neither was cake making.

A few years after the hair coloring incident, we were getting ready for the annual neighborhood street party. Mother was putting the finishing touches on her infamous cake.

"Oh, goodie!" I cheered, as if I weren't horrified at what was coming. While typically hyper-sensitive to others' perceptions, Mother was blind when it came to this cake.

It was a multi-layered sponge cake decorated in every color of the rainbow. The colors brushed on gooey and looked like they might slide down the sides, but never did themselves the favor. Mother topped it off with glistening canned peaches, cherries, and pineapple rounds.

As she placed the cake on the dessert table with pride, I caught some of the other ladies moving their lips awkwardly, stifling laughter. Mother took no notice, but Ivan did.

"Mother, those ladies keep looking at you."

Father dismissed him. "Everyone's always looking at your mother. She's a beautiful woman."

Mother's face lit up. Father was right. Mother left a lot of women in envy.

But someone muttered, "I can't believe she made that

monstrosity again."

Another whispered, "It's good to see no one truly has it all."

I felt protective of Mother. She never spoke much of her childhood, but a few times I overheard her shame for growing up poor. Although she'd never admit it, I got the sense that these women, raised in wealth, intimidated her.

I went over to the table and cut myself a big slice. I hated Jell-O—which is how the cake got its color—but figured I'd take one for the team.

Mother gasped. "Don't eat it all, Shay. Save some for the rest of us!"

But no one else dared.

As the night wore on, I caught Mother's eyes scanning the dessert table. Everything was disappearing. Except for her cake.

I did what I had to do.

Each time Mother was preoccupied talking or dancing, I cut another slice and threw it in the trash. I flung crumpled up napkins on top for good measure. And each time Mother thought she was discreetly checking on the cake, I caught her smile and turned away just in time.

The adults were getting tipsy on punch and light on manners. I overheard jabs at neighbors who weren't two feet away. Even as a kid, I was embarrassed for them.

And then someone—Mrs. Taylor—turned to Mother and said, "Well, I'm so glad you didn't let us down, Aileen. You brought your famous cake!"

Not catching on yet, Mother turned to her and smiled. "Oh! It's my pleasure!"

Emboldened by the booze, Mrs. Taylor couldn't quit while she was ahead. "Tell me, how do you make it? Do you sprinkle it with unicorn dust? Maybe bake it with faeries?"

Mother's face puckered and froze. In the background, someone giggled. Mother's head spun towards the offender, who was likely reacting to something else.

"I suppose you wouldn't know how things are made," Mother said, eyes sharp as knives. "Everything of yours is store-bought. Well, you can't buy class."

"I'm sorry, Aileen," Mrs. Taylor said. "It was just a joke."

"I'm a joke?"

"Of course not. Look, we're all having a few drinks and a good time. I didn't mean to hurt your feelings."

Mother didn't accept the apology. "Hurt my feelings? Ha! All you did was show your true colors." She grabbed Father by the arm and stormed off towards the house.

Back home, I heard her weeping and rambling to herself.

"Well, I'm sorry I can't be as highfalutin as you, Susan! You and your store-bought life—it's all out of a package or from a surgeon. Your skin's pulled back so far, you look Oriental. You think no one notices? Ha! You're as delusional as you are dumb. You know nothing about being a good wife or mother."

I told myself Mother didn't mean Oriental as an insult, but deep down understood it equated to Ugly. All Mother did was speak the truth.

The next morning I told her, "Don't listen to Mrs. Taylor. I love your rainbow cake. Everyone does. That's why there was none left."

"Just promise you'll never grow up to be such a jealous witch."

"Too bad you can't buy manners," I said, shaking my head.

Mother's face lit up. "Smart girl. I'm raising you right."

OUT OF BODY, OUT OF MIND

I suppose it's not unusual for me to have my body in one place and my mind in another. It happened all the time in school. "Earth to Shay," a teacher would snap, and I'd wake to the moment, horrified. I'd smile and mumble something unintelligible, then disappear back into myself.

"She's just so damned creative," Mother told the teachers on Parents' Night. "To be honest, I think she's a genius. They all are, where she's from. She just doesn't operate the same as the rest of us."

Because I kept my grades up, the teachers stopped asking about it. But this so-called genius of mine made me terrible at team sports. I tried soccer, softball, and field hockey. The other kids had no trouble staying focused, but I'd be on the field with balls flying past me left and right. I eventually did everyone a favor and quit.

When I tried to tell Mother that I thought I had a problem, she laughed. "You're able to focus better than most people I know. We're all different, is all."

On one hand, I loved Mother for accepting this part of me and trying to help me accept it, too. On the other, I already had enough Different. I wanted to belong.

Soon after, a synthesizer materialized in my room. "I hear you fooling around on the piano sometimes. I thought maybe you should have your own. Save the baby grand for when you're worthy."

It was the most thoughtful gift she'd ever given me. I cherished that Casio and each of the delightful, unnatural sounds it made. I locked myself away in my room for weeks, composing and arranging melodies.

Mother popped by my room one day. "See? Told you that you had focus."

"Want to hear my new song?" I was eager to share my progress.

She plopped down on my bed. And just like that, I finally had Mother's undivided attention. My nerves kicked in. I started making excuses. "I'll probably mess up a lot. I just finished writing it. I'm not sure of the chorus yet..."

"Just play the damn thing already."

I took a deep breath and sang my heart out. My fingers tripped over a few wrong keys. I tried my best to hit all the right notes. I wasn't expecting a call from Letterman, but thought I did okay.

Mother's eyes sparkled. "You wrote all those words?"

"Yep," I nodded, tingling from the astonished look on her face. For one brief moment, I felt magic.

"You should write songs for your sister to sing. After all, a voice for a voice..."

My heart sank.

It's true. Myra was one of the best singers in school chorus. She sang the way teachers like you to sing—as clear as a bell and without much emotion.

"My songs are personal. It'd be weird to have someone else sing them."

"Don't be selfish. Share the wealth. Your sister has a beautiful voice. You're obviously a gifted writer. Know your strengths."

Music meant so much to me, but maybe Mother was right: I just wasn't good enough. It seemed I wasn't good enough at anything—except coloring predictable pictures in that one boring style.

Mother left the room, and I left my body again. Hours later, I woke in the present, sitting on the same chair.

I disappeared everywhere. It happened in group situations and one on one. I was beginning to think something was seriously wrong—but then a girl at school saved me from my madness. During recess, when I was trying to explain why I'd zoned out during our game, she said, "Wait, weren't you born in March? You're probably a Pisces. Pisces are dreamers. They drift off like the ocean... or something."

It's not that I wanted to believe the stars dictated who I was. I just liked the idea of it being how I was born. That would kind of make Mother right about me. An irresistible concept.

ONE OF US

One after another, the memories roll in. I can't seem to make them stop. What good is it to re-run the past? I need to focus on the present. Get control of my body. Climb out of this sorry state.

Thankfully, I hear Jack approaching.

"There she is."

"That's your sister? She looks Asian."

"Oh, didn't I tell you? She was adopted."

A couple of chairs squeak as they sit down.

"It's kind of weird you never mentioned it," says the girl.

"I forget sometimes. She was in the family before I was born."

"How odd."

"Not to me." Jack kisses my cheek. "I brought my girl Belle here to see you. It's messed up, you being in here like this. What happened?"

"You know she can't talk back, right?"

"Yeah, but what else can I do? Sit in silence? Shay—if you can hear me—Mother misses you. We all do. We hope you'll be coming home soon."

"Is she, like, in a coma?"

"Kind of. The doctors say it's psychological. But Mother isn't sure anything's wrong with her."

"Am I missing something?"

"I think we're all missing something. Mother says she's always been happy—all the way back to when she was a kid. I take her word for it since I wasn't there, being born so much later."

"But, why would your mother know better than the doctors?"

"She's known her a hell of a lot longer. That counts for a lot when it comes to psychological stuff."

"Does it?" asks Belle.

"Mother says so."

I think back to when Jack was small. He was always so gentle and kind. I wasn't prepared to love him so much. But he wasn't like Ivan or Myra, or even Mother or Father. He was more like me—a quiet observer who liked to do his own thing.

"Must've been lonely growing up with everyone so much older."

"That's what everyone thinks," says Jack. "But I'm pretty sure I had it better than the rest. I had all of Mother's attention. There was no one to fight with. I got pretty much everything I wanted."

"Nice life."

"Don't I know it." Jack clears his throat. "That's why none of this makes sense. With a family as great as ours, no one should have problems like this."

"Well, you don't know what it was like for her," says Belle.

"We shared the same family. How different could it have been?"

"I don't know. What is she—Chinese?"

"Korean."

"Either way, that's gotta be weird."

"Nah," groans Jack. "Like I said—I always forget she's adopted. She's always been one of us. No one ever made her feel any different."

PERSONAL JESUS

Out in the hall, it sounds like someone's pushing a cart. One of the wheels is stuck. The rhythm it makes as it rolls down the hall reminds me of a song by Depeche Mode called "Personal Jesus." Whenever it came on, I thought of my father—but not because he cared or heard my prayers. Like Jesus, he was an elusive figure I was told I owed a lot to, but who never seemed quite real.

We never met our father's family. I've gathered he grew up somewhere in New England, but when I'd ask, he'd say, "Don't ask," and "This is all the family I need."

Myra says his sister died in a car accident, but I overheard Ivan saying she worked for his friend's mom. Mother said his mother was an alcoholic. The only thing I knew of his father was that he gave him a gold pocket watch.

His own family estrangement aside, he claimed, "Family is everything," and, "There's not one single person in this world who will ever love and care for you like family." I never dared call him out on the contradiction, and I never asked why Mother was estranged from her family too, if family was so important.

Being around Father was mostly uncomfortable. I never knew what to say or how to stand. Around him, the curve of my back instinctively drooped like a wilting flower. But because I was alone in my discomfort, I knew it was a problem of mine—not his.

Besides, I'm the only one who never got beatings. Myra felt it unfair and swore I was favored for being adopted. But I suspect the truth was I just knew when to keep my mouth shut. Ivan and Myra were testers. They liked to push limits. Perhaps they felt more secure in his love.

Each time I heard Ivan and Myra wailing in pain down the hall, I'd wonder why they didn't just keep quiet. It always ended with the belt or the wooden spoon.

One afternoon, a pair of men delivered a gigantic wooden spoon and fork set. "Just hang them on those hooks over there," Father instructed, as Ivan and Myra's faces filled with horror.

Mother walked by, catching a flash of their fear. She howled with laughter. "Those are just... a-ha-ha!" It took several rounds before Ivan and Myra understood the set was decorative. "They cost too much to whoop your bottoms with."

It became a running joke that one of us would be beaten with those strange oversized decorations. Because we laughed, it meant we believed in Father's limits—that he'd never hurt any of us beyond repair.

Instead of beatings, Father gave me chores. I vacuumed halls, emptied trash, cleaned windows and mirrors. He'd say, "You might think you're hot shit but we've got decades on you—real life experience. Your husband will thank us someday."

I always wondered why he assumed I thought I was hot shit. I was the weird-looking chink of the town—and only because nobody knew the word gook.

But underneath his rough exterior, Father was a softie. He

cried during the movies he called Teah Jerkahs. He surprised Mother with no-occasion gifts. He let his niece live in a suite downstairs for a year, despite his being estranged from his sister. He'd give a stranger the shirt off his back. In fact, one winter evening he came home without a coat. When Mother asked where it was, tears welled up in his eyes.

"This fella and his dog were beggin' on the street outside the office. He had on a ripped shirt and Bermudas. There was some sort of sign but it bled from the snow."

"He stole your coat?" gasped Mother. She was at the stovetop, the hood light illuminating her curious beauty.

"No. I asked him what happened—his story. And he tells me his mother died. The cancer. It was brutal, he said. And she had no insurance. So every last dime of his went towards her treatment, hoping she would survive."

"But she didn't?" Mother rested a spatula on the gold-speckled, pink Formica.

"For a few years. And every day he'd be right there with her, makin' sure she was comfortable till the end."

"What a good man," Mother said, flipping the eggplant.

"When she died, he had nothin' left—not a penny. No job, since he took so much time off to be with her. So he and his dog ended up on the street."

"Why doesn't he go to a shelter? Did you tell him about the Pine Street Inn?"

"Yeah, he knows all about the shelters around here, but it's not like the movies. You can't just show up with a dog and get help. Beds get taken. They have all kinds of rules."

"So you gave him your coat?"

"I gave him my coat and fifty-eight bucks. It was all I had on me. And the look in his eyes, Aileen. It was like I was Jesus Christ himself."

Mother beamed. "Did you hear that? That man right there is your father and you should be proud."

We gazed at him, awestruck. Because we knew the man he really was, we let him scold us and mold us. He was our own personal Jesus.

WHEN THE PARTY'S OVER

Our parents used to host the kind of grown-up parties you'd see in films. Mother hired professional decorators. There were musical performances. Father organized scantily clad girls to serve food, cocktails, and cigars.

I'd lay flat on my belly across the steps, peering down through the railing. I loved watching them when they were being people rather than parents. They were happier, funnier, and more easygoing.

Our baby grand finally got some use, with guests taking turns playing. Mother dressed in gowns with plunging necklines, knowing it was only a matter of time before she'd be draped across the piano, singing along. Sometimes she'd change outfits midway through the night. It would take a few drinks before she'd hit the floor. But when she danced, there wasn't a stray eye in the house.

Father smoked cigars in the corner with the men as the night unwound. It was awkward watching his eyes tracking the young girls' asses, but they'd always find their way back to Mother. He'd talk business and mope about corporate life, while the men slapped his back and called him Boss. Years later, I was surprised to hear people call him short, because his presence was always so large.

There were lots of good vibes flying around at these

parties. From my perch on the steps, I'd hear Mother dote over lady friends and then flirt with their husbands in ways that no one seemed to mind. She'd spend ample time with each guest, making sure they felt special. Father built up men who feigned humility, and then complimented their wives.

"If I didn't have Aileen," he'd wink and nudge. And then the man would carry on about Mother.

Mornings after would present polar-opposite scenes, leaving me wondering which version of my parents was real. Father hunched over the table with coffee and a cigarette. Mother lounging in her Oriental house dress. They'd pick at Danish pastries and each of their guests—forgetting how much they seemed to enjoy them.

"Did you see Tommy? He must've gained forty pounds. And he wonders why Linda's not interested!" Father tutted.

"Well, she's no prize. Did you see that getup she had on? Honestly... The sixties called and they want their couch back."

Father chuckled. "Mitch talks a big game but they're about to go bankrupt. He thinks we don't know?"

"That explains Jane's hair."

It was hard to tell what they enjoyed more—the festivities and fanfare, or the morning-after griping. But eventually, the parties stopped. The last must've been a few years before Jack was born.

When I asked Mother about it, she said, "Jealousy. You know? And some people just take you for granted. You'll understand when you're older. We did have some good times though—before the shit hit the fan."

"Family is everything," Father said, puffing on his menthol cigarette. "Don't you forget it. Friends will come and go all your life. They mean nothin'. What matters is who we've got here in this house."

SECRETS

I searched for secret passageways and hidden rooms. I was certain they existed. Our house was so large, a kid could get lost exploring. And maybe because of its overwhelming size, I always expected there to be more.

Who could ever truly know something that big?

I crept in closets, moved boxes, trailed fingertips along walls and floorboards. Just a crack or a hint of something unusual would spike my blood.

"What are you looking for?" Mother asked, catching me one day.

"Um… just a piece of paper I lost playing hide and seek."

I'd examine the closet in one room and rush to the other side of the wall. I'd size up the spatial constructs with a finger and thumb on my chin.

The sunlight through the windows made the house look normal—even warm. But I stayed awake nights tracing imagined blueprints in my mind, searching for something out of place; something requiring investigation.

After months of sporadic searching, I had a major breakthrough: I found the closet within the closet. It was nearly impossible to find. The closet itself was lined in wood paneling. The cracks were camouflaged.

My heart raced as I pried the door open with my

fingernails. In my wildest dreams, I imagined it would lead to a whole other world—someplace magical, perhaps. But when it swung open, I found a pallet of water, toilet paper, and energy bars.

I retraced the remaining closets in the house and came up dry. After finding the closet within the closet, I knew there had to be more.

This house held secrets. I was sure of it.

There was a crawl space at the far left of my bedroom. It opened up into another space so small I could barely fit in it. There was nothing but dust.

The attic spanned the entire house. The entrance was a ladder you pulled from the ceiling in the hallway. It's where Father stored the things that Mother didn't want gone forever.

Sometimes I'd imagine a man living in that dusty old attic. Like God, he watched us all. I pictured Father, with his generous nature, stowing him away and feeding him. Perhaps it was his one secret from Mother.

As intrigued as I was by the attic, something kept me from getting up there. If I really wanted, I could wait until Mother went shopping. But I figured I'd never get away with poking into it without repercussion. While I needed to know what was up there—every chance I had, I froze. I wasn't sure I'd be ready for what I'd find.

As strange as it sounds, somehow the attic felt almost as if it were Father's brain.

WE CAN FORGET

I just want to open my eyes and focus on something—anything—outside of myself. I can't trust that these memories are real. I never could.

My father's a saint. My mother's an angel. That's what everyone's always said. And that's what I want to believe.

Myra walks in. She sits to my right, chomping on winterfresh gum.

"Anyway, I just got my tits done again and they look a-ma-zing. The last job was okay but they were starting to sag. They said they'd never sag but I guess my skin can only hold these bastards up for so long! Oops. Is it insensitive to use the word bastard? I got high profile gummies this time, with a lift. I look like a twenty-year-old. Of course, you wouldn't care. You're Asian. You'll always look young. Even in this brain-dead state you look twenty-five."

Myra looked just like Mother before she started tinkering with everything. I think everyone always telling her how beautiful she was probably messed with her head.

It's difficult for someone like me to understand why anyone who looks like their mother—especially ours—would want to change that. But last I saw her, she had platinum blonde hair, higher cheeks, and hazel eyes.

The chair creaks as she shifts around, filing her nails. She can't sit still. She's always been so driven that when she's around, you sort of feel like traffic in her way.

"Graham just signed a big contract with Target. He's going to be in all the TV and print ads." Her third husband is over a decade her junior.

"From the moment I saw him, I knew he could be a big deal. Now that he's finally got an agent worth his cut, things are happening. He'll bring in a good chunk of change, but it's the recognition we want. Once he's made a name for himself, he won't need to kiss up to anyone."

If I could move, I'd be nodding my head. She doesn't need much encouragement, but if you don't react once in a while, her eyes go cold.

"We might try to get pregnant once these puppies heal up. I'll get a tummy tuck post-delivery. I know I'm on the older side but now that my window's closing, I'm afraid I'll miss out. Adoption's always an option but—you know more than anyone—it's not quite the same."

It stings. Not that I prefer Mother's utter denial, but Myra takes such pleasure in delivering the burn.

"I bet I'll look better than all those young dumb moms anyway. Graham and I would make beautiful babies. Don't you think?"

There's no doubt in my mind they'll make perfect little figurines, like the ones Mother collects.

"Everyone else is doing fine. Daddy's quiet. Mother's still unnerved about your being in here but pretends not to be. Ivan and Jack are charging ahead. People won't fucking stop asking about you. If you get out of here, we can throw you a party. You're more popular than ever."

Myra shifts in her seat and sighs.

"Mother and Daddy are renovating the kitchen. We're

going ahead with Andrei's party. Ivan's stressing out because it has to be perfect. And, of course it will be. You're missing out on all the fun."

There's a break in the nail filing for a moment, and Myra's silent.

"You know, Mother refuses to visit because she knows you're doing this on purpose to embarrass her. Everyone's talking about it. But if you're trying to hurt her, you're failing. She's stronger than you think. You have no control."

I want to say, look at me. Does this look like control?

"Mother says your online groups are probably responsible. She says you've always been creative but you'd never get this idea on your own. I tried logging into your Facebook and email accounts. I may have locked you out, not that it matters."

This shouldn't surprise me, because Mother's always spied—supposedly for my own good. But it's interesting that she's rallied Myra for help. She's never needed assistance.

"Well, Shay… I can't spend all day here going along with your act. I'll leave you with this: If you get out of here, we can forget it ever happened. Daddy and Mother agree that's the best way forward—so we can all move on. Ivan and Jack are down with the plan."

Myra's heels click as she rises to her feet.

"We can forget it the second you walk through that door. You don't have to be afraid it's too late. We love you, you know."

As Myra leaves, I wonder what love means to her.

TROUBLE

Myra claims it's not true, but there were a few years when she and Mother didn't get along. It started when I was around seven or eight, so she would've been twelve or thirteen.

One of Mother's few lifelong friends, Erica, was visiting. The two of them were gossiping and sipping cocktails in the living room. Mother's eyes always looked so blue when she drank. It never ceased to amaze me.

I was reading a book in the corner of the room when Myra proudly emerged. She wore a petal-pink mini skirt with a studded white belt and a colorful heart-patterned half-shirt. She twirled in the center of the room.

Erica's eyebrows went up. "Ho-ly shit. Aileen, you've got trouble."

"I don't know where you think you're going in that getup, but you're dead-wrong unless it's to your room to change," Mother said.

"It's Clarissa's. She's allowed to wear it. We traded a few things for the week." Myra failed to hide the pleased flush Erica's words had given her.

"Oh, let the girl have some fun," Erica simpered. "You used to dress like that. In fact, you look the spittin' image of your mother, Myra. When she was young, she turned heads like no other. Till you, that is." Erica laughed and took the straw from her glass, tipping her head back to slurp up the last of her drink.

Mother kept quiet until Erica left, and then gave Myra hell. "You look like a tramp! I don't know who this Clarissa character is, but you're done with her. And when your father gets home, you'll be sorry for the way you acted today in front of Erica. How dare you back talk me like that? Do you want people to say I can't parent my kids?"

"I didn't think you'd get so mad!"

"You didn't think at all, as usual! It's a damn good thing you're pretty, but pretty won't get you everywhere."

"I'm sorry!" cried Myra.

"You will be."

And she was right. Father took off his belt that night and whacked Myra's back until she stopped crying. Then he started again, until she wailed deeper than before.

But the thing about Mother is you could never stay mad at her. No one could.

Later that night, I saw her go into Myra's room with mint chocolate chip ice cream and hot cocoa overflowing with marshmallows. "I'm sorry that you needed to be punished. One day you'll learn what it's like to be a mother and how you sometimes have to do hard things out of love. Now, eat this. You'll feel better. Besides, you need to put some meat on those bones. The emaciated look is out."

A week later, Mother was cutting up watermelon in the yard. A gentle breeze swept her fiery locks into a dance. The hot summer sun caught the blade of the knife, and her eyes twinkled.

Myra's hair was piled on top of her head. In a seafoam-green floral bikini, she rubbed suntan oil into her skin. She glimmered like a mermaid leaping out of the water.

I was pumping my legs feverishly, trying to see if I could get the swing to loop all the way around. The kids at school said someone's brother did it.

Father was manning the grill, cooking up marinated cow and chicken.

"Ivan, help me out here," he hollered.

Ivan, still on his board, skated towards the grill.

"What's up?"

"Get the ones that are ready into the buns and then throw these on."

The boombox in the grass by Myra commanded everyone to "Wang Chung." I had a deep loathing for that song. It inspired kids to karate chop in my face while I rolled my eyes with a smirk, so not to be dubbed humorless.

I was just about to flip the swing over the top when I heard Father tease Myra. "Somebody has boobies!"

"Stop..." Myra whined.

My legs froze, and I glanced over at Mother, whose eyes were wide open. She pressed her lips together tightly as her face turned the color of her hair.

"Somebody has boobies!" teased Father again, tickling Myra as if she were an infant.

I peered over at Ivan, who was grinning and half-heartedly flipping burgers. "When are you going to grow some boobies?" he asked.

I pumped my legs again—as if the swing could float me straight out of the yard. At that moment, I begged the god I wasn't certain existed to never let me grow boobies.

Mother began chopping pineapple more aggressively.

Thwump! Thwump! Thwump!

"Ted!" she yelled to Father.

"I'm busy, hon."

"Well, I'm glad you're so busy because I've just sliced my finger off!"

Everyone flew into a panic, tending to Mother. Ivan got the car running. Myra threw Mother's severed flesh and some ice into Tupperware.

Myra and Ivan sat in back fanning Mother as Father broke traffic laws.

We waited in the ER for hours. But as luck would have it, it was only the fleshy fingerprint that was maimed.

FAMILIARITY

In the next room, a young girl counts in Chinese and I'm suddenly reminded of Chia Ling.

A Taiwanese family moved into town when I was halfway through the fifth grade. One of the girls was in my class. We looked enough alike for white people who didn't know us to assume we were sisters.

I suppose I've always been envious of families who resemble one another. I longed for that visual reassurance of belonging.

Chia Ling taught me to count in Chinese and how to eat ramen with chopsticks. I showed her how to wear oversized socks and pretended to know about American boys. She was amazed at the idea of an Asian girl growing up in a white family. I was amazed at the idea of an Asian girl growing up in an Asian family.

As we entered a new school in the sixth grade, Chia Ling and I launched into full-on twin mode. We chopped our hair into the same China Doll bob and began coordinating outfits.

The girls in our class thought Chia Ling was cute. I was a little jealous of the positive attention she received, despite us looking so alike in their eyes. The thing was, she was more foreign than me—which made her authentic. I was caught in the limbo of No Man's Land. As Chia Ling adopted some of my accent and I took on some of hers, we slowly morphed into one.

Being part of a pair, I suddenly didn't mind the attention my Asian appearance garnered, because I no longer felt so alone. In the white suburbs of Boston, I was going to have an audience no matter where I went. It was nice to finally share the stage.

Because her family's apartment was so small, we spent all of our time at my place. The first time she had me over though, the jig was up. Her mom and aunt discovered Shay Stone was the name of a throwaway Korean—not the wealthy white girl they assumed her to be.

The next day, Chia Ling swung by my locker with a drawn face. When I asked what was the matter, she said, "My mom says we can't be friends anymore."

"How come?"

"Because you're not American enough."

My face burned. I'd known how it felt to be snubbed by white people. But till then, it never occurred to me that I might not be good enough for other Asians.

Mother was livid with That Chinese Lady. She hated the idea that some poor, foreign woman who raised five kids in a two-bedroom apartment with her sister thought her daughter wasn't good enough.

"I clothed and fed that girl," Mother grumbled to herself as she cleaned. "Just who does she think she is? My daughter is every bit as American as the next."

But the thing was, I wasn't quite.

Mother must've read my mind. "You are American. You became a citizen when you were three." She enunciated each word as if English wasn't my first language.

The next day, she sent me to school in a freshly bought

dress that was red, white, and blue. It was humiliating.

"When Mrs. Lu and her sister come to walk those kids home, you make sure they take notice. Walk with your chin up, real proud—and let them see you get into the limousine."

I did what was asked of me but it didn't make a difference. Chia Ling began to avoid me in the halls, and we both diverted questions about why we were no longer speaking.

I didn't talk to Chia Ling after that, but the following year a miracle occurred.

SHAE

We were leaving a rest stop convenience store in Vermont when in walked another Asian girl with a white family. Mother couldn't stop herself. She jumped in front of them and said, "Hi! Is this your daughter?"

"Sure is," said the father. "This is our son Aaron and our daughter Shae. Shae was adopted from Korea."

Mother's face lit up. Motioning towards me, she told them, "This is my daughter Shay and she was also adopted from Korea!"

Their eyes ping-ponged between us, and their mouths gaped. Mother frantically motioned for me to join them. I reluctantly did.

"What year did she arrive?"

"'79. Yours?"

"Unbelievable! '79!"

It felt like they could've been talking about cars.

The adults swept us together, encouraging us to exchange numbers. We traded awkward smiles on our own.

Although I first cringed at the idea of two adopted Koreans thrown together, Shae was the best friend I'd always wanted. I finally knew someone who shared the same perspectives on the world and the way it viewed us.

Since Shae lived in Vermont, for a couple of years we'd

take turns staying weekends. We slept in the same bed and even showered together, marveling over our differences and similarities.

Life just seemed easier with Shae in it. All of the things we'd never been able to articulate traveled over the phone lines with ease. With her, I truly felt understood. We shared how it felt to be a spectacle everywhere we went with our white families. We'd report how the boys would tug at the corners of their eyes and ask if we had sideways vaginas. I confessed that, not understanding what the kid meant when he asked if "down there" was the same as our eyes, I'd said yes. We had laughter instead of confusion and tears.

But as always in life, something happened to fuck it all up.

It was the summer in between middle and high school. Shae was staying with us for the week. Our house had four showers, so I couldn't understand why Mother was so upset that Shae was taking so long in one of them.

Mother loved Shae. She'd take us shopping and out to lunch. When people would ask if we were twins, she'd eagerly tell our story to the rapt audience. People were amazed by the beauty of our chance connection, and charmed by Mother's turned-up adoration. But on this day, Mother despised Shae and everything about her.

Shae emerged from the bathroom in a towel. Father was just entering the hall.

"You're lookin' grown up these days."

Shae smiled politely and let him pass before crossing the hall to my bedroom.

Later that night, as Shae and I were at the kitchen table eating dinner, Mother appeared. She was holding Shae's yearbook in the air. "This is disgusting! Just what kind of monsters do you associate with?" Mother flipped to a drawing made by some boy at Shae's school, and shoved the book towards us. It was a Picasso-esque likeness of a penis between breasts.

Ivan laughed maniacally, but Mother didn't scold him.

Shae dropped her fork. "Um, what are you doing with my book? That's my private stuff."

I was both proud and afraid.

"Excuse me?" Mother said. She widened her stance. "This is my house. There's no privacy in my house. I have a right to anything in it."

Although I was used to Mother going through my things, I didn't expect her to go through a friend's.

"Whatever," sighed Shae, picking up her fork again.

Mother was livid. She stormed out of the kitchen to find my father and holler at him.

After Shae went home, she called me. "You're not going to believe this, but we can't be friends anymore. Your mother got in a fight with my dad. She said I was a bad influence and I'm not allowed to talk to you. She even told him they should check me into juvie. He laughed at her, thank God."

"This is over that drawing."

"Yeah. I still can't believe she went through my stuff."

"I can. There's no privacy here." My cheeks were so hot that I thought my head might explode.

"So, my dad said to tell you that your mother's gonna check the phone records to make sure this is our last call. I don't know… Maybe we can use payphones or something. But it's bullshit."

I could hear the pain in her voice. I wanted to be the kind of girl to say fuck it, she can't do that—like one of the brave kids who stood their ground in books and movies. Shae was the best thing that had happened to me. But there was just no going up against Mother.

We managed some sporadic calls from payphones but eventually lost touch. Before cell phones and the Internet, it was too hard to stay secretly connected.

WE DON'T OWE

All the friendships that were taken from me, I was never allowed to grieve.

"They don't matter," said Father. "Family's all that counts."

"Stop moping," said Mother. "You have so much. You should be ashamed of yourself for ever feeling anything but grateful."

And I was so ashamed. I still am. But on some level, I don't think I should be.

Weighed down by my grief, Jae-Mee comes and lifts it for me.

"No word from your mother yet." He kisses my cheek. "Paisley still cries for you every day."

We sit in silence. Basking in his quiet presence transports me to another time and place.

Jae-Mee and I connected through our adoption, but we first bonded over Prince. We were acquaintances, milking our last drinks at the tail-end of an adoptee event. "When Doves Cry" came on and we both moaned, "I love this song."

"I used to listen to this on my headphones when my parents drove me crazy."

"It's just epic," Jae-Mee beamed. "He's one of the greatest."

"A true genius."

"So much better than MJ."

"Way!"

Soon after we started dating, a black cat showed up at Jae-Mee's window. He put up signs and checked for microchips, to no avail.

"What should we name her?" he asked, with the cat's little head tucked under his chin.

"I always thought the name Paisley would be cool."

"Then she'd be Paisley Park," he said, given that his last name is Park.

"Wow. That's perfect!" I laughed.

Months later, Jae-Mee asked me to move in. The three of us became a family. I thought our adoptive histories would bond us deeply, but we couldn't really go there. His experience of being raised in a Korean American family was too different from mine. We had other things, though— beyond being adopted and our shared taste in music. We were kind to each other in a way that, like never before, felt right.

"The place feels empty without you." His baritone voice pulls me back to the present. "Cooking for one is no fun. Can't imagine what it's like for old folks when they lose their people."

At this moment I decide that I can't be angry if Jae-Mee moves on. Wasting his life on loyalty to a two-year relationship wouldn't be fair.

"Well, I guess it's a good thing you can't talk, because I brought your journal." He gives it a spank. "I'm kind of hoping I might find a clue or something. Figure it's a little less wrong if I only read it in here with you."

I scribbled in a paper journal after yoga. My real diary's behind a locked blog online. Mother's curious nature taught me to guard my innermost thoughts.

Jae-Mee flips through some pages. "Huh. No dates. Okay, we'll do this roulette style." I picture his thumb like the arrow on a spinning game wheel, as the flipping pages slow to a stop. He clears his throat.

"We're supposed to serve one another. The beauty in life is in how we make others feel. It's our job to help others. But what if the way to make others feel good hurts us? Is that the ultimate gift—the gift of ourselves? The sacrifice we make out of love? And what if the way to make ourselves feel good hurts others? Is that selfish? Or is it what we deserve for our own suffering?"

Jae-Mee closes the book. The chair squeaks as he readjusts himself.

"I guess we'll always have to do some things we don't like—laundry, things at work... But we don't owe anyone our suffering, Shay. That's what I think anyway."

Jae-Mee's thoughts on something that's plagued me for most of my life seem painfully simplified. I can't imagine a world where it actually works that way. Even my adoption was suffering—I suspect for both my birth mother and me. We suffered to give the Stones more love. And isn't that beautiful?

"You know," Jae-Mee whispers, "I kind of wish we talked more about this stuff. I remember you'd say things like this and I'd change the subject as fast as I could. I was out of my depth. Talking about feelings seemed to come easy to you and I sucked at it. But maybe it would've brought us closer. And maybe you wouldn't be in here."

THE ACCUSATION

When Mother was pregnant with Jack, I wasn't too happy. I wasn't worried that a baby would usurp my role in the family. I was afraid to witness her unconditional love for a baby who was truly hers. But I didn't let any of this turmoil show on the outside.

She was at her worst when she was pregnant with him. The late months were during the most relentless heat of the summer. I did what I could to avoid her when we weren't out in public, where she always shined.

That was the summer I started to experiment with makeup. I was a late bloomer, and could never get anything right. Eye shadow was devoured by my flat monolids, as I hungered for the dimensional beauty all around me. My barely there lashes pointed straight down no matter what tools I tried.

One day I was able to make it all work with a little pink lipstick and charcoal eyeliner. I was feeling okay about the face in the mirror for a change, thinking maybe I could start high school off right. Mother was walking by when I stepped into the hallway.

"What the hell did you do to your face?"

"I'm trying something different."

Mother stepped forward, taking my chin in her hand.

"You're ruining your looks. Do you want to look like one of those Vietnamese whores? Wipe it off."

"Why? Myra's been wearing makeup since she was younger than me. All the girls at school have been wearing it for years. I just want to look normal!"

"Well, you're not normal—you're Korean, and you look terrible! I'd be embarrassed to take you anywhere. Get that shit off your face! It doesn't work for you. And while you're at it, wipe that smirk off, too."

"I'm not smirking."

"Oh, no? I see you right in front of my face! You know, I really hate who you're becoming!"

"You're so mean!" I instantly regretted it.

The rest happened so fast. Mother lunged at me and I twirled, backing out to the hallway. She pushed and pushed and I lifted my arms to my face. I don't know how it happened but she fell back against the door and hit the wall.

Clutching her head, she shouted, "She hit me! That little shit hit me!"

My jaw dropped and my heart pounded in my throat. I was speechless.

Ivan and Myra came charging out of their rooms.

"You hit your pregnant mother? What the fuck's wrong with you!" Ivan screamed, smacking me so hard I heard my neck crack.

"I-I didn't! I was just trying to defend myself!"

"You're unbelievable," hissed Myra. "What an ungrateful bitch!"

"I didn't do anything!"

Ivan shoved me. "Don't you dare call Mother a liar. And don't you touch her again or I'll fucking kill you myself!"

Mother quivered in the doorway of my room. Ivan

steadied her. "Come on. I'll make you some tea. Do you want something to eat? Let's get your feet up in the parlor."

Myra stared daggers at me as Ivan helped Mother down the hall.

I slipped into my room, shut the door, and collapsed face-down on the bed. I wondered what just happened. Replaying the scene in my head, none of it made sense.

Did I hit her? Or is she losing it? It all happened so quickly, but I couldn't have hit her. What kind of person hits their pregnant mother?

I was frozen somewhere between my world and theirs. And I felt so completely alone in mine that I let myself drift back towards them.

I suddenly felt sorry for all of my failings; for everything I was and couldn't help but be.

THE HOT GIRL

No matter the turmoil at home, things always settled as if they had never occurred. And so I moved on as best as I could so not to be left behind. I feigned normalcy at home and at school.

Vera was the most popular girl in high school. I'd known her since MacArthur Elementary. We always sat near each other in homeroom because both our last names began with S.

She had chestnut brown eyes that somehow matched the highlights in her silky caramel locks. Everyone adored her body. She was beautiful and looked mature. I liked Vera because her life intrigued me. And I suppose a small part of me wanted my family to see I had popular friends.

Her mother was a single parent. She was a sharply dressed businesswoman, and none of the other moms seemed to like her. There was a rumor that she slept her way to the top, but she never struck me as that sort of person.

We were hanging out in my room listening to "Cars that Go Boom" by L'Trimm when Ivan barged in. Vera and I were lying on our stomachs and Ivan took a long, lingering look at Vera's ass.

"You staying for dinner?" he asked, tilting his head up and peering down his nose.

"Yeah," I answered for her. "Why?"

"It's ready in five minutes. Don't be late." He leaned on the doorframe for a moment before leaving.

"What's his problem?" Vera asked.

I shook my head. "He's lame."

Father was smoking a menthol cigarette at the table. His eyes traced Vera as she moved through the kitchen. I wished he would've tried to hide it, but it's like he was oblivious to his obviousness.

"You like burgers?" Mother asked, fixing our plates.

"Yes, please," Vera said politely, as if she were addressing royalty.

"One or two? Cheese or no?"

"Dairy makes girls big-busted," spoke Ivan. The rest of us pretended not to hear.

"One with cheese, please. Thanks, Mrs. Stone."

"You see?" Mother glared at me. "She eats burgers. Why can't you?"

I rolled my eyes and kept my mouth shut.

"Just fries for you then?"

I nodded, stacking lettuce, tomatoes, onions, and pickles on my plate.

"Save some of that for the rest of us," snapped Mother.

"You in the ninth grade?" Ivan asked Vera, his mouth full of burger.

Vera nodded.

"What's the matter? You mute?"

"Sorry, my mouth was full."

"Um… Boner."

"Ivan," warned Mother, with a sigh.

"I'm a senior in college," he said. "Northeastern. You look like you could be in college."

"Well, she's not," I said.

Mother was bottle-feeding Jack. "Don't mind him." She smiled at Vera. "Ivan's always had eyes for the pretty girls."

Vera lit up for Mother. "It's probably because you're so pretty."

"Oh!" Mother fluttered, patting her chest. "You're too kind!"

It was the sort of exchange I witnessed at school. The pretty girls were always patting each other with niceties and responding with synthetic humility. They'd look around, tallying witnesses to this approval.

After dinner, we scurried back to my room. Vera laid on my bed, her pose accentuating the impressive curves of her body. I wondered what it must feel like to be so white, womanly, and beautiful—exactly what the bulk of the population lusted after or wanted to be.

"Your father was staring at me," she said, reaching back to stretch her dancer's thighs.

"He does that," I mumbled.

"Why?"

I shrugged.

"And what's up with your brother?"

"He likes to make people uncomfortable."

"He's good at it. Remind me to never sleep over."

I could feel my face redden. Ivan always had to put on the Perv Show. And why couldn't Father be more discreet?

"Your mom's awesome, though," she offered. "It's hard to believe she just had a baby. I hope I look as good as her someday. Maybe I'll dye my hair red."

Changing the music, I nodded. "She's pretty great."

THE ATTEMPT

So much remembering of what I've tried to forget makes me queasy. I've felt nauseated since I've been in here, trying to make sense of it all.

Dropping into the past again, Mother said, "Let's just forget it ever happened," while tying my hair back with an elastic. "We all have bad days and do stupid things. There's no need to make a big deal of it."

I could barely keep my head up. I rested my chin on the toilet bowl rim, unfazed by stray pubic hairs and other debris.

"Myra!" Mother hollered, propping me up. Her voice sounded like it was coming from inside a tunnel.

Myra ran down the hall. "What's wrong?" Her voice sounded far away, too.

"I need some help making her throw up."

I was tired and wanted to sleep. My head was spinning, but I couldn't do the one thing she begged of me.

Myra paused. "Uh… And why do you think—"

"We don't have time for that crap. We need some help, now!"

They tilted my head back and poured warm salty water down my throat. I choked, coughing it up, but they forced some more down. Myra handed me a toothbrush, handle first, and said, "Touch as far back into your throat as you can, then press."

I gagged, but nothing came up.

"Drink some more of this," said Myra, pushing the glass into my mouth so fast that it clunked against my front teeth.

"She hates meat," said Mother. "Go microwave that leftover steak from the fridge."

I chugged the salt water and gagged harder, but only thin bile came up.

Myra returned with that God-awful smell, broke off a piece of steak with her hands, and shoved the tough flesh into my mouth. I recoiled, but Mother held firm.

"Chew and swallow! Just eat the fucking thing!"

"Why don't we take her to the hospital?" asked Myra.

"That's not going to look good for her, is it? Mrs. Anderson works in the ER. Do you want her daughter to tell the whole town that she tried to kill herself?"

Mother was right. I didn't want to draw any negative attention to the family. So I pinched my nose, chewed the cow meat, and swallowed. I sucked down salt water and the marathon puke-fest began.

Mother patted my back. "That's it. Get it all out. Pretty soon it'll be over and done with—a thing of the past."

After another two rounds of feeding and puking, they helped me to my room. I climbed into bed and hugged the covers tightly, shaking. On the inside, I shivered. On the outside, I sweated. Deep, sharp pains dragged through my stomach. My head pounded like it was inside a kick drum. There was a sizable egg growing on my forehead. I must've fallen before Mother found me.

I was allowed to stay home from school, and was left mostly undisturbed in my room for days. Sometimes I'd emerge to use the bathroom, or fetch a glass of water and some Saltines.

Nobody questioned what had led me to such a desperate act. In a way, I was glad—so I just let it go. All that remained in my chest was regret. I didn't have the motivation to sit upright. I didn't distract myself with cable and couldn't focus on books. I just lay there like a big sorry lump.

"What were those pills, anyway?" I asked Mother, when I was starting to feel better. I'd swallowed half a bottle that I found in her room.

"It doesn't matter," she snapped. "Let's forget it ever happened. All of that's washed away now." She forced a smile. "You're lucky I found you in time—and that your sister knew what to do. Your sister always seems to know how to take care of herself without bothering anybody. But it's okay. We saved you. Again."

Like always, Mother's smile managed to light up my heart and tuck away my own pain.

I smiled and nodded back robotically.

I went to the crabapple tree in the yard. Sometimes I liked to stretch underneath it and test my fate, wondering if the sour fruit would drop on my head. At the right time of spring, yellow-green leaves filtered the sun but I could still see the sky. Lying there, warmth returned to my face, and my stomach felt fuzzy. I think I felt loved.

DISBELIEF

"Shay, enough with this shit." The sound of Myra's voice jolts me back to the present. She throws her bag on the chair to my right.

"I can't believe you're still doing this. How much pity do you need? All right. We get it. Poor little Shay was angry with Mother. Big deal. Grow up already."

She paces back and forth, heels clicking in threes.

"I told you—all you have to do is get up and out of this shithole. Quit faking. We're ready to move on as a family. Don't you want to be part of it?"

All I've ever wanted was to feel like part of the family. It surprises me to hear Myra ask as if it were up to me.

"What you're doing is a slap in the face to everything we've done for you. We brought you to America. We took you in and treated you like one of us. We've saved your damn life time and again. Remember?"

How could I forget?

"You're ruining this family! You're killing your mother! Don't you care?"

I hear her exhale heavily through her nose. And I know somehow she believes everything that she's saying.

"What do you want? Just sit up and tell me. I'll do whatever's in my power to make it happen."

I want to tell her it's not in her power.

"Sit up! God damn you! Sit up!"

Myra shakes me. Her hands grip my shoulders and hot air streams from her nostrils.

"Why won't you sit up, you stupid bitch? You're ruining this family! My God—you're so stupid! Get up!"

The machine I'm attached to starts beeping fast and irregularly.

A nurse storms in. "Get off her! Out! Now!"

Myra continues to shake me, raining tears on my face.

"You don't understand! She's faking! She's ruining our family!"

More footsteps rush in, and Myra's torn from my body.

"You're banned from here!"

"Yeah?" Myra snarls. "Good luck with that."

As the beeping slows down and steadies, I realize I'd completely stopped hearing the machine at some point. It's only when it changed that I noticed it again. As time marches on, it fades from my awareness once more.

GOOD TIME

Lucky and Saved had a brother named Guilt. They followed me wherever I went.

I've had crippling stomach pains for as far back as I can recall, and I swear it's a gift from Guilt. Things I should've said and done better—they take on little personas and sit around a bonfire in my stomach toasting marshmallows as I pray for death.

They loved to visit during long car trips. On drives to our regular resort in Vermont, like clockwork, the pain would trickle in around the forty-five minute mark.

"Jesus, Shay! What'd you eat?" Father yelled at the rearview mirror, catching sight of me flopped forward. I was in so much pain that I couldn't speak.

"It's the dairy," insisted Mother. "A lot of Orientals are allergic to dairy. Did you eat cheese? You know not to eat cheese."

Cheese doesn't give me stomachaches, but I didn't protest.

"Maybe you should pull over at the next exit," Mother said. It warmed my heart that she went to bat for me.

"I'm not stopping till we hit the halfway mark."

"I have to poop!" squealed Jack.

"Go in back!" shouted Father.

Father loved Jack but by the time he came along, I think

parenting had lost its luster.

Jack let out a long, melodic fart as he climbed over the back seat of the van and opened the lid of his plastic potty. The van jumped over a bump in the road. The smell ripened in the air.

"This is fucking mental!" shouted Ivan.

"If you kids don't pipe down..." Just as Father's fist hit the wheel, the van swerved and sirens blared from behind.

"Pull over, Ted," urged Mother.

But he kept on driving. "Everyone just shut the hell up!"

Eventually we stopped and sat a few minutes, waiting like cornered prey.

"I need someone to wipe my bum!" said Jack.

"Not now! Jesus Christ." Father looked in the rearview mirror, shook his head, and muttered through his teeth. "You kids."

As the policeman approached, something twisted in my stomach and I truly believed I might die.

"Everything okay?"

"Yes, officer."

He peered in. "What's wrong with her?"

"Sit up, Shay," Mother said sweetly.

I inched up just enough to make eye contact. I thought, great. He probably thinks I'm the reason for the smell.

"Our daughter has a stomachache," said Father.

"She's adopted," added Mother, as if that were somehow important.

The cop nodded. "I'm going to need you to step out and open the back."

"Uh oh!" squeaked Jack.

Myra started to laugh. Mother shot her the look of death.

Stone-faced, Father climbed out of the van and shut the

door behind him. They walked past my window to the back. As they flung the doors open, Jack began to cry.

"My son's potty training."

The cop sighed. "He shouldn't be in a moving vehicle without his seatbelt."

"It was an emergency situation. What am I supposed to do? Build a seatbelt into that thing?"

"Look, you've obviously got enough going on without a ticket. Get him belted in before you get back on the road."

"Thank you, officer."

I was still keeled over in pain but wouldn't dare make a sound.

"I need to be wiped!" cried Jack.

"Quiet!" Father warned, getting back into the van. "You almost cost me a fortune. Your mother will clean you when we get to the place."

"But that's hours away," Myra said.

"Not another word."

The lid was shut and the windows were cracked open, but the stench wouldn't fade. No one dared complain, but the looks across our faces said it all.

After ten or fifteen minutes of silence on the road, someone's laughter broke through. And then another cracked. Hell—even I, with my crippling pain—joined the mad chorus.

We were one disaster after another. We didn't laugh together often, but that day we laughed for nearly two hours. It was crazy, but I almost felt like I belonged.

CHINESE-LOOKING GIRLS

I was moping around the kitchen looking for something to eat, but gave up, afraid it would make me fat. I was growing more conscious of the difference between my body and the white girls' at school. They all looked like tall, thin supermodels while I looked like a Yukon potato dropped down five flights of stairs.

"What's the matter with you today?" asked Mother.

"I'm fat and ugly—just like every other day." I slumped over the table.

"You are like fun. All of my kids are beautiful."

"I hate the way I look. Why'd I have to be born looking like this?"

"Because you're from Korea."

Silly me! I must have forgotten!

And then my father chimed in. "When I was young, I used to think if I could just get my hands on one of those Chinese-looking girls…"

"Thanks a lot!" Mother's face went red, and she pressed her lips tightly together.

I wanted to escape to my room, but felt too uncomfortable in my body to stand.

I couldn't understand Mother's offense. Everyone knew she was beautiful. No one could hold a candle to her—let alone her weird-looking adoptive daughter. Yet somehow Father's words managed to upset her.

"Why don't you unload the dishwasher," said Father. "Make yourself useful."

As I rose, Mother stormed out of the room.

When I unlatched the door, steam rushed to warm my face. The hair that I so carefully curled and sprayed fell limp across my forehead. Although I hated this task, there was something rewarding about the burn of hot ceramic mugs on my hands as I bent over and stretched to put them where they belonged.

"You're built like a brick shithouse," murmured Father, smoking his menthol cigarette. "There's nothing wrong with the way you look."

I pretended not to hear him. My body forgot how to move. Every bend and reach felt exaggerated. I was ashamed of the ways I had to maneuver to get the job done. It felt like hours of agony—like I was forced to do a striptease for my father.

After finishing my chore, I nearly tripped over my own feet walking past him. I made my way out of the kitchen, not wanting to be asked to do any more jobs. All the while, I felt guilty for hating his company. I went to my room and collapsed on my bed.

Myra sparkled when Father complimented her. I never took compliments well. I always ended up feeling ashamed.

NO NORMAL GIRL

Mother always said that the truth doesn't matter; it's what we learn from the situation.

I used to spend a lot of time in a world-renowned music producer's studio. I met his kids at the Boston Music Awards, which a friend had invited me to. My goal was to have this producer discover me so I could garner the fortune and fame to make Mother proud. It was the least I could do to pay her and Father back for adopting me.

I wasn't especially talented. Not all of his groups were, but they had the look and he taught them how to act. I figured he didn't have any Asian groups, so maybe if I were around enough he'd get the idea on his own. After all, I was great at pretending.

Someone told me that he watched me sing and play piano once, but he must not have thought I was pretty or good enough. I still held out hope that the next time I'd be prettier and perform better.

The only problem with hanging out at the studio was dealing with the producer's brother. He was a middle-aged man named Marvin who drank and smoked and openly flipped through nudie mags. He knew I was friends with his nephews, but liked to play hardball.

I rang the bell and knocked on the door.

"Who dat?" Marvin asked, peering out through the blinds.

"It's Shay."

"You can't come in."

"The boys are expecting me."

"Well, they ain't done. You're gon have to wait out there."

"Marvin, it's sketchy out here."

"What? You 'fraid some black folk gon get ya?"

"Just let me in, Marvin."

This happened every time. And every time the door would eventually open and Marvin would fume while I sat waiting for the boys to finish up. This one time, though, I waited around for what must've been hours. Every now and then I got up to pace, peering up the staircase. And then Marvin rose and pinned me against the door.

"Quit playing around."

"Who's playin'?"

"The boys will be down soon. You'll get fired."

"Naw, I'm in through blood, see. Now, who are you but a little rich girl from the suburbs? Always comin' down here in your fancy ass clothes and shit, waitin' to play with the little boys. What's wrong with the men?"

"I'm fifteen," I said, figuring it would sway him. "Let me go."

"Not till you let me put my hand down your pants." He snickered.

"Ha ha, very funny."

But he jammed his hand straight down the front of my jeans and started wiggling it around.

"Quit it," I barked, trying to squirm out of his grip. But he was three times my size.

"Oh, you got that nice tight Asian pussy."

"I'm going to scream if you don't stop."

"No you ain't 'cause if you do, I'll snap that pretty little head off ya."

I shut up and let him do what he had to do. He never took my pants off to do worse, so I suppose I was lucky.

When he finished, I stormed out of the studio and walked until I found the subway station.

"Last train's gone," said the man in the booth. "Just missed it."

"Shit," I groaned, heading for the pay phone.

When my parents' limousine pulled up outside the station, a window rolled down to reveal two sets of eyes, round with horror.

"Get in the car," Father hissed. "You want us to get mugged or shot?"

Mother was quiet but her face spoke volumes.

I climbed in and silently stared out at the inner-city night. Mother rolled down the dividing window. "Are you going to tell us what happened or what?"

"I was waiting for Charlene to finish her take." Charlene was a sixteen-year-old white soul singer. I knew she'd sit better in their minds than three black teenage boys. "I fell asleep in the waiting room and lost track of time."

"So you walked all the way to the station in the ghetto alone at this time of night?" Father narrowed his eyes in the rearview mirror.

I nodded.

"If you'd have gotten killed, you might've deserved it."

"I hope you got a good scare," Mother added.

Too stubborn to let Marvin keep me from my potential success, I went down to the studio twice more. I arranged for the boys to meet me outside around back. I'd wait under the stairs with my back against the bricks, practicing songs in my head.

"Why don't you wait inside no more?" one of them asked.

"I don't like Marvin."

"Marvin? He's fine."

"He stuck his hand down my pants and said he'd kill me if I told you," I blurted.

"Nah ah."

I nodded.

"Bullshit."

"I swear."

"If that were true, you'd never have come back. Don't be spreadin' no rumors like that. Damn."

I never spoke to the boys or went back there again.

I told myself it must be true that no normal girl would risk putting herself back in that position. So, why did I?

DEAR MOTHER

A woman gave birth to me, but I was told not to consider her a mother of mine because mothers are the ones who raise you. Mothers are the ones who never leave.

The mother who raised me always leaves. But it's always been my fault.

Mother and I stopped talking a few months back, after the following email exchange:

Dear Mother,

I've been trying to make sense of some things from my childhood lately and thought maybe you could help.

Remember when I tried to commit suicide and you found me on the bathroom floor? I was wondering... Why didn't we go to the hospital? I'm also curious why you didn't think I needed therapy. I was depressed for a lot of my life—which is nobody's fault. Probably just my own faulty wiring.

Anyway, hope you don't take any of this the wrong way. I'm so glad to have you as a mother. I can't imagine having been raised as anyone else's kid.

Love you,
Shay

Days accumulated into weeks with no response. My heart

sank each time an email notification arrived and it wasn't her. I picked up the phone several times on the verge of calling, but chickened out. And then finally, twenty-three days later, I received this:

Dear Shay,

You were always a happy kid. Despite a few dips here and there, you were beautiful, popular, and well-adjusted. I have no idea where this suicidal business came from. As far as I'm concerned, you were a normal thriving teen who just had a short lapse of common sense. I wasn't about to ruin your reputation over it.

Maybe you'll see for yourself someday how hard it is to be a mother. I did everything I could for you kids and when I ran out of steam, I found more ways to love.

I loved you the moment I saw your picture. I always told you that. When we picked you up at the airport, you were the prettiest and quietest of the bunch. We were so proud of you. You were always smarter and more talented than your brothers and sister. They were jealous of what you could do.

I've recently heard from Myra's old best friend. She wrote to tell me how happy she was because she now has four kids of her own and she always wanted to be like me. Now she is.

I also heard from Ivan's old friend. He wanted to thank me for all the dinners and sleepovers, and being everything his own mother couldn't. He said he treasured all our talks and the shirts I bought him. True stories for what they're worth.

So if you're calling my parenting into question, maybe you need to take a hard look at yourself and those around you. Maybe whoever is putting these ideas in your head has some sort of ulterior motive? Perhaps they can profit from your pain? Whoever it is can't possibly know me or our family based on a few one-sided anecdotes you may have told. And that's why I never advocated for therapy. They don't do anything but blame the parents and drag you through the past.

My advice to you is to stop looking back. You won't find answers there. The only way is forward.

You'll always be my daughter. Xx

That afternoon, I responded carefully:

Dear Mother,

Thank you for writing me back. I'm sorry if I may have unintentionally accused you of being a bad parent. You and Father were wonderful parents. I never meant to imply that you weren't.

But I don't understand how you chalk my suicide attempt up to a temporary lapse of judgment. What about all those letters you found and burned in the sink? While it's true that I had a lot of happy moments as a kid, I was also really depressed. Maybe you didn't notice because I didn't want to upset you?

Anyway, I'm not blaming anyone but myself here. I was just hoping you could shed some light on your decisions so I could get a better sense of how things were. As you've always said, I tend to remember things wrong.

Love, your daughter,

Shay

Despite following up, I didn't hear from Mother again.

Mother was right. They always blame it on the parents. I quit working with my therapist, Dottie, as I felt it was partly her fault. In my short time with her, she kept bringing the conversation back around to Mother, despite my insistence that my troubles were on me.

Digging through the past is dangerous, since one can never truly know or remember. I created a beast and dragged it into the perfectly good present without any means to tame it.

Mother feels things deeply. She always has. Her sensitivity is a double-edged blade: One side butters and the other side cuts.

So, Mother won't be visiting—not today and not ever.

DARK ROOM

It seemed like I went from ugly chink to object of desire overnight. Boys who had either taunted or overlooked me suddenly saw me in a new light. Sometimes I'd excuse myself from class to examine my reflection in the bathroom mirror. I didn't look any different.

I thought of Shae and wished I could call to see if she was experiencing the same thing. But I didn't dare risk it showing up on the bill—and it'd been so long since we spoke. I kept it to myself. It's not something I felt comfortable discussing with anyone else.

Some of the girls in photography class started asking if I could model for them. It was both uncomfortable and refreshing. I never dreamt anyone would want to take or see pictures of me. To my surprise, they got passed around and random students would compliment me on them in the halls. But I remained skeptical of the attention. I was certain that at best, I was a fad that would fade.

Aside from the increased popularity, photography gave me a sense of purpose. I'd wander for hours on end, re-examining everything around me. I was creating my own world, highlighting what went unnoticed. I told myself that was probably why my classmates wanted to take my picture—not because I was beautiful, but because they'd never seen me in a flattering light. And maybe they liked the challenge, too—making something appear more special than it was.

Thursdays after school became my usual time slot in the dark room. We'd sign our names on the calendar taped to the door. Two were allowed in the room at a time, but Thursdays were empty. I could spread out my work, taking over the drying line.

Tucked away, I was finally free to do my own thing. I could explore at my own pace, and make mistakes without fear. There was no one to scold me or stop me.

I was zooming in on the reflection of a tree with a pair of ducks floating in it, when the door opened and closed. I thought nothing of it, focused on getting the crop right. When I didn't hear anyone moving around alongside me, I glanced up to see who it was.

Keith was a popular jock. He played three sports and dated cheerleaders. I never thought he'd noticed me. But there he was, standing before me with his pants down.

It took a moment before I could find my voice. When I did, all I could say was, "What are you doing?"

"What does it look like? Wanna give me a hand?"

"I'm busy. You should leave if you're not developing anything."

"Who says I'm not developing anything?"

I gathered my negatives, leaving my ruined prints behind. But as I moved to the door, he blocked me.

"Let me go."

Keith grimaced and shook his head. "Keep working if you want. Or come help me out."

"I'm leaving."

"No you're not." He leaned against the door.

I was afraid to turn all the way around in case he came at

me. So I went to the far corner of the room and partially averted my eyes, keeping him in my peripheral view.

He moaned louder than I'd expected as he brought himself to climax. To be honest, despite being afraid and disgusted, I was fascinated by his moment of vulnerability. There was something disturbingly intimate about it. It made my skin crawl.

Taking a wad of paper towels, he cleaned himself up, said, "Thanks, doll," and left.

Keith never asked me to keep it a secret, but I was afraid to tell anyone. I figured it was a one-time thing. When he'd pass in the hall, he'd shoot a knowing wink, sending chills down my spine. I hated it, but on some perverse level I also enjoyed the attention.

The following week, I was working away in the dark room again, certain lightning wouldn't strike twice. I'd taken shots of random things around the house that I wanted to make abstract—like Mother's old house dress hanging in the back of her closet. While rotating and framing the golden embroidery, I heard the door open. I looked up right away, hoping for another student or teacher.

Keith stood, undoing his pants. "Want some more of this?"

"No. Why are you bothering me?"

"Lift up your shirt."

I shook my head, backing away slowly. I wasn't sure how far he was willing to go this time and was nervous to find out.

"Lift up your shirt or I'll come over there and stick it in your ass."

"Just please, let me go. You don't even know me."

"Last chance." He smirked.

My back hit the wooden shelves, and I reluctantly lifted my shirt up just over my sports bra. Although the tightness flattened me out, without a shirt on it created cleavage. I was thankful that was enough for him. He pulled at himself until he climaxed.

"Nice choice in lingerie." He turned to leave. "Till next time."

Once he'd been gone a few minutes, I sat down on the cold floor and silently wept. I asked myself why I didn't float off to another world during these times, but couldn't make sense of it. I didn't wallow in my sadness or questioning, though. I gathered my things and refused to be rattled too long.

I stopped developing pictures at school. I dropped my uncropped negatives off for fulfillment at the shopping plaza and finished out the semester with a B-.

BETRAYAL

There were times I swore my sadness and anger would devour me whole. Like a dark, heavy blanket, it smothered me. All of my energy went towards feigning normalcy in a tough trade for a slice of peace.

Loneliness crept under my skin and swam through my veins. I felt like a defective product without a warranty or place of return.

Sometimes I'd wander the streets at night. It was quiet in the suburbs, with very few people to fear. Listening to loud music on my headphones sure beat trying to tune out Mother at home. It seemed she was always angry, too—threatening Father with divorce. And then Jack would start crying and even in a house that large, it was hard to hear my own thoughts.

The good news about Jack taking up all of Mother's attention is that she didn't bother with me anymore. I was thankful for the reprieve, but in a strange nagging way, I missed mattering.

Junior year, I started sleeping with boys. I knew I was nothing more than an exotic curiosity to them, but in a twisted way, I enjoyed being wanted. After a lifetime of feeling I couldn't measure up, I didn't mind the objectification so long as I was the one in control. I objectified them, too. They were nothing to me but an outlet for my self-esteem and racial frustration.

And then out of nowhere, I fell in love.

I was at the movies with a girl I'd recently met at a party. She was an average-looking girl with enormous breasts that were always on display. Her bouncing boobs caught a couple of guys' attention as she shook flavoring onto her popcorn. They headed our way.

"What are you ladies up to tonight?" asked the blond.

Angie grinned haughtily, pushing her chest out even further. "Hanging with you."

"Nice. We've got tickets to Trainspotting."

"Same as us."

"All right. Let's go get some seats. I'm Michael."

As the two of them walked arm-in-arm into Theater 7, I trailed behind with Brandon, the dark-haired kid.

"I've never seen anyone like you before. Where ya from?"

"The next town over." But I knew what he really wanted to know.

"Before that?"

"Korea."

"Yeah? North or South?"

"Supposedly South."

"But you're not sure?"

"Fucked if I know."

Brandon smirked. "You a tough girl?"

"Only when I have to be."

Halfway through the film, I saw Michael with his hand down Angie's top. He kept squeezing and roaming her vast breast-scape. I jabbed Brandon with my elbow. He peered over and we snickered together like children.

Three-quarters of the way through the film, Brandon's

hand found mine. Our eyes met, and I thought my chest might explode. There was just something about him that brought me to life. Although he was a decent-looking guy, I'd been with cuter. His effect on me defied explanation.

After the film, we went to Michael's house. His parents were away for the weekend, so we did shots of everything in their liquor cabinet.

Brandon and I shared cigarettes on the couch while Michael and Angie loudly enjoyed each other in the next room. We played Truth or Dare.

I chose, "Truth."

"How many guys have you slept with?"

"Six. You?"

"Zero."

"Zero?"

"Yeah, I don't swing that way."

I threw a cushion at him. "How many girls?"

"Forty."

"Really?"

"Nah. Just four."

"Serious?"

"So serious. Can't you tell by my serious face?"

I laughed. "You look like a serial killer."

"Out of the six, who was your favorite?"

"I don't know... Maybe number five."

"Why him?"

"Because he was one of those kids who made fun of my face when we were little."

"Shouldn't that make him your least favorite?"

"No. It was more like, 'Not so ugly now, am I?'"

"What is that—like, revenge sex?"

"Maybe. But then I guess it was all revenge sex."

"All the times you slept with him, or everyone you've slept with?"

"Everyone I've slept with."

"What's with all the vengeance?"

I shrugged. "Everyone thought I was hideous until all of a sudden, they didn't."

"I can't imagine you were ever hideous." He said it in a way that made me want to believe him.

But I told him, "You must not have a very good imagination."

"Truth or dare?"

"Dare 'cause this party's starting to get boring." I yawned.

"I dare you to kiss me."

Straddling him on the couch, I kissed him for two hours. His hands never left my back and mine never strayed from his face. Strangely enough, we were both quite content.

Brandon and Michael were similar in build and wore their hair the same way. They could've passed for brothers—and acted as such—with Michael as the bossy older one.

The four of us became a regular thing. We never explicitly said it, but I began to consider Brandon my boyfriend—my first love. His green eyes, dark hair, and slightly muscular body quickly became my world.

We spent a weekend at Michael's cottage in New Hampshire just before school started back up. I took a part-time job at a warehouse so I could buy clothes, including a cute bikini, without Mother knowing. It was my first trip away with a guy and it took everything I had in me to play it cool.

The cottage was rustic and charming with gingham linens and handmade furniture. It was right on the lake, allowing for night swimming, drinking, and stargazing in rowboats. The setting was so romantic that it was hard to feel grounded in the present. I felt as if I were in one of those novels for housewives.

There was a big tree outside our window that blacked out our room at night. Michael's cottage didn't have a candle or night light so I had to be a big girl and deal with it. But I had Brandon to protect me, and I was beginning to feel safe with him.

The second night, we were exploring each other's bodies in the dark. "We already know what we look like," said Brandon. "Not being able to see kind of makes you feel more. Doesn't it?"

Giving my body and mind to the moment, I couldn't help but agree.

Just as I was about to climax, Brandon paused and said, "Shit. I've gotta pee. Be right back."

"Hurry," I pleaded.

Feeling piqued and alive, I fluffed the pillow and spread out into the center of the bed.

"That was fast," I said when he returned.

He hushed me before slipping back in. He lifted my legs in a way he never had before and I started getting into it. It felt amazing. And then I got the strangest feeling that something wasn't quite right.

"Brandon?"

He shushed me, thrusting even harder.

"Brandon?"

"Quiet," he whispered, pumping his body into mine.

"You're not Brandon!" I screamed.

And he climaxed at the same moment.

"You're not Brandon!" I repeated. "Where's Brandon?"

Suddenly, he was out. The door opened and the lights flicked on, blinding us all. The two boys stood with towels around their waists.

"What the hell's going on?" Michael shouted.

"That was you!"

"What are you talking about?"

"That was Michael. Wasn't it, Brandon? Tell me the truth right now!"

Angie entered the room. "What the fuck, guys? What's with the shouting?"

"Your boyfriend was just inside me!"

"No, I wasn't. You're crazy. She's crazy!"

"Say something, Brandon," I begged.

But Brandon just stood there. "Guess I'll sleep on the couch," he finally said.

"You can't even say it!" I yelled. "Wow. You can't even say it was you because you know it wasn't! Why aren't you mad? Wh... Were you in on it?" I could hardly believe the words coming out of my mouth.

Brandon left the room and Angie backed out behind him.

Michael smirked, leaning against the wall. "Why don't you get some rest. You drank too much and you're acting crazy." He shut the door and walked away.

Outside the room, I heard Angie's voice. "Is it true? Did you fuck her?"

"No. She's crazy."

"Because I was wondering where you were. Figured you were in the bathroom."

"I was in the bathroom. Jesus Christ. I won't be accused of this shit in my own fucking house. Now, enough."

I didn't speak to anyone the next day. Brandon's silence was even more telling than his eyes. When he dropped me off at home that afternoon, I fixed him with a hard stare. I never heard from or saw him again.

REGRETS

I think sometimes we tell ourselves we had no choice when we're not proud of the choices we've made. And sometimes we make the right decisions but don't have the courage to see them through—so we cite them as mistakes.

Because I'd just plain had it with life, I gave up on people and bought art supplies. I stayed in my room painting piece after piece. I had no idea what I was doing, but that didn't stop me. I picked up magazines from Chinatown and blended cutouts of Asian women with chaotic layered painting techniques. Kids and teachers would ask what they meant, but I don't think I realized I was working out my frustrations with being an Asian girl in white America.

My art teacher loved my work so much that she was adamant I apply to art school. I kept trying to tell her that Mother wouldn't have it—I needed to study something more lucrative and prestigious.

"Besides, this is all I've got," I told her. "It's not like I have a variety of styles and inspirations."

"Art school will bring it all out in you. You have a gift that most of us wish we had. Don't let it go to waste. Go. Live on campus. Get the full experience. Otherwise, it's just not the same."

As I'd predicted, Mother wasn't having any of it. She was

angry with me and livid with my teacher. She even called Ms. Rainer to say, "I'm not paying for her to learn how to teach kids to make silly pictures! Stop putting ridiculous ideas in her head!"

But Ms. Rainer wasn't intimidated by Mother's rage. Instead, it motivated her to help me get my portfolio together and research scholarships. "Despite your family's wealth, your work and your grades should get you in." And with her glowing recommendation, I was awarded a full scholarship with housing included.

Of course, Mother protested every day for the rest of senior year. She stopped buying the vegetarian food I liked and cut off my art supplies fund. But when she discovered I took a job at a gas station, she had the manager fire me and threw a wad of cash on my dresser.

"I will not have my daughter pumping gas. People will think we've gone broke."

Myra cornered me in the hall one afternoon. "You're not really going, are you? After everything she's done for you?"

I sighed. "It's the only thing in life that I actually enjoy."

"You're such a selfish little bitch. Don't you think Ivan and I have things we'd like to do? Do you think we'd still be living here if leaving wouldn't totally crush Mother?"

"Those are your decisions to live with or change." As I walked away, she threw her bag at me.

The truth is: I was scared to death. I was afraid of defying Mother's wishes and living away from home. But Mother had been cold to me for so long that I'd forgotten how it felt to have something to lose. In a way, I'd been grieving the loss of Mother's love since that day I colored outside the lines.

Another truth: At the time, I had no idea what it'd truly be like to grieve Mother.

Everyone in the family declined the invitation to my graduation. No parties were thrown and no cards or gifts were given—all because of art school.

Mother stormed into the room while I was packing. She leaned over my suitcase, removing articles of clothing she'd bought me and throwing them into a pile on the floor. "And that suitcase is ours, too." She dumped the remaining clothes on the bed and picked up the suitcase.

"That's fine. I'll get my job back to pay for a new one."

She threw the suitcase at me and left my room, slamming the door.

I stopped in the kitchen before heading out to my cab. "I'm leaving now."

"You'll regret this," Mother said. "Mark my words. When you're teaching little brats how to glue construction paper for twenty thousand a year, you'll realize your mistake. And by then, it'll be too late. You'll have to start over. Who'll pay for that? Don't come crying to me."

I walked out the door.

Behind me, I heard her shout, "Good riddance, you ungrateful little witch," followed by the sound of glass breaking. But I didn't look back. I gave the driver my portfolio and suitcase and sat in the backseat, tears gathering in my eyes.

UNSPOKEN LOVE

Art school was everything I could've wanted it to be, if only I could've been someone else. The students seemed to know who they were, and wore their identities with pride. It was obvious that they didn't belong most places, but they belonged there. Together.

There were more than a few other Asian faces in the city. And they often had Asian last names. They had Asian friends. They joked about being in Asian families with—sometimes derogation, but—an unspoken love.

One of these true Asian Americans was in my conceptual drawing class.

"Hey. You Korean?"

"Kind of."

"Hapa?"

"Adopted."

"Oh. So, like, you don't speak Korean or anything?"

I hadn't even eaten Korean food at that point. I shook my imposterous head.

"Ever been?"

"No," I said, feeling the heat in my cheeks.

"Oh."

And that was that.

I couldn't find my place. I loved the projects, but missed

out on all of the bonding I saw taking place everywhere else. No one knew what I was supposed to be. And neither did I.

Benjamin was the first person to show any real interest. We met in 2D Design class in the second semester. As soon as we started talking, I felt like I'd known him for years. There was just something familiar about him—as if we could've known each other in a past life.

Charismatic and doting, he was always center stage. People flocked to him because he made them feel good. It was hard to believe that he chose awkward me.

Things were great for a while. I was, without a doubt, at the heart of his world. He wanted to spend every night together, and every moment outside of class. It was starting to interfere with my work.

A few months in, I tried to explain. "I might just need a few hours to make some progress on my conceptual piece."

"Sure. Let's go to the studio together." Seeing my expression, he asked, "You don't want me to come?"

"I love being with you." I put my hands on his waist. "But it's hard for me to focus when you're around."

"It's 'cause we have so much passion." He swept me into the air and showered me with kisses.

"I know. And I love it. But I need a little space to—you know—try to make something good."

"We make something good." There were stars in his eyes. He was irresistible. So, after we made some more out of our passion, I let him tag along.

It was nice to feel wanted—especially since my family was still hanging up on my calls and ignoring my emails. Ivan and Myra only communicated to tell me I was rotten. And Jack was just a kid. They didn't recognize my birthdays or invite me to holiday gatherings. I even missed Ivan's wedding.

Benjamin's intensity filled the gaps and overflowed. It felt like the love I had always been craving. I stayed with him during school breaks. We went on weekend excursions with his friends. When it was good, it was great. But his jealousy was hard to bear.

If I was laughing with a guy at a party, he called me a slut. When I snuck away to get some work done, he'd be suspicious. He didn't trust me. And it got to the point where I didn't trust him. But each time he saw me reaching my limit, he reeled me back in with his charm. We went on like this for a year.

The night I told him I wanted to break up, he slapped me across the face and kicked me in the stomach when I fell to the floor. He spit at the ground before heading out to a party—where he told all his friends that I cheated on him with two guys at once.

I was devastated. It was hard to believe that someone who had claimed to love me so much, was capable of causing me so much harm. Everywhere I went, one of his friends was there to call me a whore or vandalize my paintings.

And in this devastation, I texted Myra: I think I made a mistake.

She fed me back my own words: Well, it's your choice to live with or change.

It didn't feel like much of a choice. Staying felt like dying and leaving felt like dying. But on top of what happened with Benjamin, Mother's continued absence was true death. I couldn't take it anymore.

Instead of exploring the museums in Europe with my classmates at the end of sophomore year, I turned up on Mother's doorstep. She glanced down at the suitcase. "Welcome back." She was not the hugging type, but her half-smile was all that I needed.

Leading me in as if I were an old lodger, she said, "Ivan and his wife have taken over a wing. Your room is just as you left it."

GHOSTS

Sometimes it feels like I'm underground and the living stop by my grave. I imagine it's easier to confront someone when they're a symbol, unable to respond.

Benjamin stomps into my room. For a skinny man, he's always been heavy-footed. He says he wants to "pay his respects." I've never heard of doing that with the living.

"I know it all went south between us but after all this time, I've never stopped thinking of you. I cyber-stalked you a little and saw what you've been up to... before this. You did alright after dropping out of school. I haven't gotten anywhere. I'm still a fucking bartender. Can you believe it? Nobody wants original illustrations. It's all stock art these days."

Classic Benjamin. Despite all his privilege, he's always the victim.

"Saw you're with some Asian dude now. Hope he doesn't have anything to do with this."

My heart stops. I wonder how many others might wonder the same. Jae-Mee, the first gentleman I've ever dated, doesn't deserve it.

"You know, I may have been a little overprotective," he says, with a sharp shift in tone. "I never should've hit you. That was shitty of me. But you weren't perfect either. Your drinking was obnoxious. And you never gave me any respect.

You took me for granted."

A few women hover by the door and weep. They won't come in, like I've got a disease they might catch. I'm unable to place them.

My Godmother pops in. "I just found out yesterday. I'm sure you know I haven't spoken to your mother in decades. I'm sorry I stopped sending cards. I was warned not to, but I shouldn't have listened. Well... It breaks my heart to see you like this. If you find your way out, let's have lunch—on me. I'm sure there's a lot to catch up on."

It's hard to know for sure that these visits are real. It could be the drugs that swim through the tubes and into my veins. Or I could be like Ebenezer Scrooge, visited by the ghosts of my past.

Whatever happened to Onward and Upward, Don't Dwell on the Past, and Happiness is a Choice? The How to Live clichés scroll through my brain, reinforcing my failures.

The last morning I remember being fully awake, I posted on Facebook: "Life is 1% what happens to you and 99% how you react to it." That's how I wanted to live—with the illusion of control. And here I am, a non-functioning catatonic. It feels pretty big for 1%, but all those Internet memes can't be wrong.

For my 35th birthday, Mother gave me a book on The Law of Attraction. The first rule was: Don't Ask to Understand Why You Suffer. Take Steps that Seek Joy and Celebration. I broke that rule with my email to Mother, which led to our latest estrangement.

The second rule was: Fake It Till You Make It—this is an area in which I excelled.

Rule Three was: Take Action, or Walk the Walk. I made cards for my family with poems describing the closeness I longed for. It felt satisfying on some level. But something was missing.

Rule Four: Be Open to Answers and If You Think Your Question Wasn't Answered, You Weren't Paying Attention. I found this one antagonizing. It made me want to run face-first into a cactus.

The Law of Attraction is about mind control. While there are some things about it that make sense to me, it sets my brain on fire. I've tried to control my thoughts and feelings to maintain a positive outlook. And look at me now. In the end, my sadness leaves me feeling like a bigger failure for not being strong enough to stop it.

Perhaps it's what landed me here. And perhaps it's why I need ghosts.

LIVING THE DREAM

Living back home with its old comforts felt undeniably right and incredibly wrong. My longing for family and Mother was somewhat soothed. And the desire to explore any potential I may have had was completely crushed.

I didn't want to paint anymore. I could not bring myself to pick up a brush. It felt like a betrayal to Mother. I needed to find something else—something good enough for us both.

None of the listings in the paper seemed worth pursuing. I was unqualified for anything interesting I found online. Tempted to talk to Mother about applying to a more academic program, I remembered her words as I left for art school. I didn't want to give her a chance to throw them back in my face. And then, miraculously, the perfect opportunity arrived at my feet.

Mother was updating some legal documents, so she hired an appraiser to examine her estate. Afterwards, as they sipped tea, I overheard the woman say that her husband had a design firm in the city. It had been so long since I'd heard Mother boast about me. "My daughter Shay just spent a couple years in art school. She got a full scholarship—for the prestige, of course. Obviously money wasn't a problem. But, you know, she was so disappointed by the experience that she came home. The truly gifted can't learn in those environments. If your husband's ever looking for someone of her caliber, I'll put you in touch. I'm sure it'd be mutually beneficial."

A couple of days later, I met with this man whose name was—I shit you not—Art Starr. With salt and pepper hair, he was dressed to kill in an impeccably tailored suit and converse sneakers. Surrounded by trophies and awards, he looked pleased with himself.

I felt like a total sham, standing there in Myra's dress and Mother's jewelry. I mimicked his posture and tone, and acted like they'd be fools to pass me up. I was sure he'd see through it and send me packing.

"How's sixty thousand to start?" I assumed his smirk meant he was joking.

"It's okay but I was hoping for seventy." I started to rise, figuring the jig was up, we'd had a laugh, and it was time for me to leave.

"Done. People have to know their own worth. You'll go far, kid." He winked. "See you Monday."

Mother was overjoyed by the success of her maneuvering. She demanded we celebrate over dinner. She and Father made cracks to the servers about how their big investment was about to pay off.

Myra, who'd just ended her brief first marriage, sulked at the end of the table. "Where's my big fancy job?"

"Oh, Myra..." said Mother, shaking her head. "Brains are not your department. Keep at the modeling. You'll catch your break."

"I mean—why can't you meet the head of a modeling agency who'll book my breakthrough? It's hard out there for models my age. I'm competing with teenagers, for God's sake. I told you—I should've started sooner. But you wouldn't listen."

Mother thought a moment. "Maybe Shay will have a chance to choose models at the new job? You'd hire your sister, wouldn't you?"

"What? I don't know if I'll be in charge of those things."

"You'll help your sister however you can," said Father. "That's what we do in this family."

"Of course I will if I can." I twisted my cloth napkin on my lap.

"Tell them I'm a model, actress, and singer. I'll give you some cards to keep on your desk."

Myra had plenty of cards but not many jobs. Casting agents always said they were seeking the girl next door. Ironically, that's exactly what Myra had morphed away from in an effort to be star material.

Mother delivered five bags of high-end clothes to my room. "You'll need to look the part. It's more about appearance and fitting in than anyone wants to say, but it's just the damn truth."

I wanted to tell her I understood that better than she could imagine.

The first week was mostly making decisions on my benefits package, watching videos on privacy policies, and filling out legal forms. The second week, it became clear that I had no clue what I was doing. People were put in charge of training me, much to their dissatisfaction. But by the fourth week, I was able to translate my ideas adequately into digital form—and Art Starr was pleased.

He took me to a fancy lunch the day we heard back from a happy new client. He bought a one-hundred-dollar bottle of wine and ordered for me. When I said I was a vegetarian, he laughed. "You'll grow out of that." So I picked at the side dishes and listened to the colorful tales of his big wins throughout the years.

Lunch lasted the afternoon. Before I knew it, he was ordering dinner—along with another bottle of wine. I started to worry what people back in the office might think. He asked what I thought of his wife, and advised me not to settle down for another fifteen years. "Men are more valuable married. Women are more valuable single."

Mother wasn't keen on my arriving home late, but quickly changed her tune when I shared my first success story. She poured us some wine, despite my objections. I gave in and was glad that I did, because it was the first time we sat together to celebrate something I had done. I felt like we'd come full circle. I was a toddler again, making her proud by just being me.

In my drunken delight, I told her, "I'm going to pay you back—for more than just the clothes. For all the food and diapers when I was a baby, the opportunities, and letting me live so well."

Mother sat there with the light dancing in her eyes. I flashed back to that day I spied her singing along to Elvis when I was a small child. Buzzed from the wine, my chest tingled upon realizing that this was the moment I'd been waiting for to arrive.

With her hands resting on her chest, she said quietly, "I knew this day would come. I'm so proud."

THE WRONG PATH

I set up an automatic transaction for every paycheck to deposit 20% into Mother's account. It was the simplest way I knew to give back.

Mother said, "Of course we don't need the money. I'll add it to your inheritance."

I told her to use it as she saw fit. It felt amazing to be able to contribute financially after a lifetime of feeling indebted.

Discussing my day and the office dynamics over wine with Mother became a regular thing. She was riveted by all the politics, chiming in on the inevitable workplace drama.

"Reminds me of my modeling days," she'd eventually say, followed by a story that wasn't quite relevant but made her happy to recount. I basked in the privilege of closeness. "I always wondered what I might have become," she confessed one night.

"Why'd you quit?"

"It's not a life that sustains you. It's a lot of long hours and catty women who are all jealous of each other. And the agents and designers are so controlling of how you look all the time. I did it as long as I had to. It was fun being invited to all the big events. I knew it would land me a good husband and an easier life."

Sometimes Myra would stop into the parlor. "What—

you're BFFs now?"

"Don't be jealous, Myra. It doesn't suit you," Mother said. "See? It runs rampant in the modeling biz."

But the longer I was at my job, the more demanding it became. Meetings took up the entire day, and the actual work didn't start until four o'clock. I'd arrive home later and later—cutting into my time with Mother.

"Work/Life balance is important," she'd warn. "Don't let them take advantage of you."

"It's just the industry." I was hearing stories of how things worked all over the city. "People expect to pull all-nighters if it lands them new clients. Some even sleep in the office. I may have to get a place in the city."

Mother's mouth dropped open. "Maybe this is too much for you." She downed her wine.

"I don't mind it. It's almost like this is what I was meant to do. It comes easy to me. I enjoy it."

"But is it the life you want? To be a workaholic with no time for yourself or your family?"

"My coworkers say it's just what we've gotta do. We're lucky to earn a good living this way. They pay a lot because they expect a lot."

"As an adult, you'll face a lot of forks in the road. Think hard before venturing too far down the wrong path."

A few weeks later, when I sat down with Mother, I had to tell her the truth. "I'm exhausted. It'll be easier if I rent a place near the office. I can stay there during the week and come home on weekends."

"You're going to throw good money down the drain every month on some dingy apartment when you can stay in a mansion for free?"

"Well, I can afford it easily enough. The benefits will

outweigh the cost. I'll be able to go home for naps while I'm waiting for files."

"Is this job really worth it?"

"Don't you think? I'm meeting interesting people and working with talented artists. Each year, our work gets submitted for awards—which looks great on resumes. And there are a lot of big names. You'll be able to walk through stores pointing to brands I've worked on. Wouldn't that make you happy?"

Mother sighed. "Of course it will, but we'll never see you. Any job that takes so much time away from family messes with priorities."

"But I don't have a family yet. Shouldn't I build my career now while I can and worry about that when I do?"

Mother's lip stiffened. "How dare you? After all we've done for you all your life..."

My heart raced. "I didn't mean it like that."

"You have a family, Shay Nari Stone." She stood up. "The trouble is, you forget what it was like when you didn't. Go ahead then. Move out if that's what you want."

"You know that's not what I meant. I never said—"

"Save it. You've said enough." She stormed out of the room.

Mother refused to speak to me while I waited for my lease to begin. After I left, she'd hang up when I called. When I rang the doorbell on weekends, no one answered. And so began the second time Mother—and the others—disowned me.

STILL NOT MOTHER

I've lost all track of time. The longer I'm here, the harder it is to decipher what's real and what's imagined. Did that nurse sponge-bathe me a few hours ago, or was that yesterday, or last week? Did Jae-Mee come to see me again? Or was that a dream?

You're gonna make me lose my mind. Up in here. Up in here.

I think it's already gone.

For my darling, I love you. I love you. I love you.

For my darling, I love you... and I always will.

Promises, promises.

What good is a promise, anyway?

Promises are the naive human desire to create permanence in an ever-changing world.

Promises are manipulations to gain something in return.

Thoughts are like waves crashing into each other.

If you love someone, set them free.

The ones who give up their children are the ones who love them most.

I can't remember the last time I heard Mother say she loved me. Mother only said she loved me when she was telling the story of how she loved me before we'd met.

I may die as motherless as I began.

Was it pride? Ego? Stupidity?

What did you do, Shay? What did you do?

If I could go back in time, I'd whisper in the ear of my past self. I'd tell her the true meaning of Gratitude and Living in the Present. I'd warn her of the dangers of Dwelling on the Past and going against Mother's wishes. I'd explain that life is too short to disappoint those who have high hopes for you. I'd let her know that nothing is worth the pain of being estranged from your Forever Family.

Caving in to Mother may have felt disappointing, but this is worse. This isolation, this lack of defense—it's far worse. Isn't it?

Listen to me, hung up on my mother at thirty-seven fucking years old.

If I could Houdini myself out of this place, I'd scroll through all the Facebook posts that tell you how to live, and share them as if I were in on their truth. Mother would Like each and every one. She'd comment how I made her proud in ways that would somehow garner more Likes than my post.

If I could go back, I'd live life knowing it's not all about me. I'm just a bit part in the play. My job is to help others shine.

Sometimes when I hear footsteps in the hall, they sound a little like Mother's. Like a dog left tied to a post, I wait on high-alert for what never comes.

Other times I imagine I've gotten my vision and legs back. Like nothing, I rise and walk straight out of here. Outside, the sun catches Mother's hair. I run to her with my arms open wide, but her face morphs into a stranger's when I reach her.

My legs ache from imagining running as fast as I can back to Mother.

GOOD FORTUNE

Many gloss over the pain of an infant denied its one true need: their mother. Too many adoptees are instructed to erase that pain because it doesn't serve the narrative of being saved. It gets in the way of Not Dwelling on the Past and the Feel Good Story the World Wants to Hear. And it gets in the way of how we want to feel—which is grateful, strong, and in control.

In the right hands, a child who has been shot through the heart with an arrow might be saved. But each day as he showers and dresses, will you tell him not to notice the scar? Will you deny him his right to be fearful of arrows? If he is, does that mean he's not grateful for life?

Any one of us could have been aborted, died at birth, or passed away within the last minute. How grateful are you? How much gratitude is enough to wash away any pain you might have?

Finding my people was like being in a desert for decades and looking up to see thousands of people rushing towards me with food and water. For a while, I was obsessed. I wanted to meet everyone and learn everything. I interacted with my new friends online several times a day, and eventually got involved with a local group. Like with Shae, we just understood each other. With them, I felt like I belonged.

But it wasn't always perfect. Once the high wore off, I

started to see where things were disjointed. We seemed to be divided into groups: those who praised adoption, and those who spoke critically of it. In these groups, I spoke highly of my family and all they provided. Despite our estrangement, I mimicked verbatim many of Mother's words—how fate brought us together and that my adoption meant I was wanted. It felt nice to reinforce the sentiments that made others feel good.

Weeks before I ended up in the hospital, someone bared her soul. She spoke of her father's abuse—from age five through twenty-five. Now her father was sick and she debated not visiting him. People told her:

"Be the bigger person."

"Don't be stubborn. You'll regret it and can't take it back."

"Grow up. We all go through shit. He's your father, adoptive or not. Everyone makes mistakes."

"Do the right thing."

"You owe it to yourself to love him more than he loved you. Don't let his behavior excuse your own."

If there's one thing people on the Internet love—besides food and cats—it's to dole out advice; the less solicited, the better. But people often make judgments based on their own experiences. It's difficult for anyone—even the most well-meaning—to comprehend an ugliness they've never endured. And sometimes the subject's too close and they're not ready to look in the mirror.

I sat back and watched the advice pouring in. Sometimes I just wasn't in the mood to debate the validity of my feelings. I watched the original poster defend herself. I read how badly her father beat her and the terrible things he would say. And then I watched as person after person dismissed her pain.

People wrote posts complaining about how the negative

posts brought them down. They boasted of their own positivity. Many laughed at the Ungrateful Adoptees for Dwelling on the Past and refusing to evolve.

"You must live in the present!"

"Be thankful you didn't grow up in Korea on the streets!"

"Hey fatty! You'd have starved to death if your parents hadn't adopted you."

"I know a girl who was abused in the orphanage she was raised in. At least during your abuse, you were given a good education."

Sometimes the biggest pain is caused by those you imagine are like you—only you find out that life treated them better.

Someone posted a meme that said: "I flood my brain with positive thoughts so there's no room for the negative." It got two hundred and seventy-eight likes.

Someone else posted a school bus. The left side of the image was black and dreary. The right was sunshine and flowers. "It's Your Choice Where to Look. We're All on the Same Bus." It got three hundred and twenty-four likes.

Many of my people have endured worse things than I have. I wasn't beaten daily. I wasn't home-schooled by my abuser. I had my own room with a window. I had art supplies, a synthesizer, and my own computer.

I was sad for the others, but thankful for my good fortune. And so I showed up at Mother's door with a smile and bouquet of flowers—not to move in, but to visit. She let me back into the family for another short while.

KOREAN BARBIE

"Good news!" Jae-Mee bursts in, followed by a second set of footsteps. "I convinced your family not to do electroshock therapy. They didn't read the articles and stuff I sent, but before they could hang up on me I told them people would blame them if it went wrong—and boom! It worked."

"Why aren't you her healthcare proxy?" asks Amanda.

"She's been at the same job for a long time. I guess she never bothered changing it on her health plan."

Amanda's another local KAD—Korean Adoptee. She looks like a Korean Barbie. If I'm honest, I've always felt myself shrink in her presence. But she was never anything but sweet to me.

"Hi Shay. Sorry for being a shitty friend." She pauses. "I was sort of afraid to see you like this. Jae-Mee was nice enough to bring me with him. You look... good."

And that pause is hard to gloss over. I'm suddenly conscious of my appearance—not that I can do anything about it.

"A lot of people are asking about you," Jae-Mee adds.

"I saw your kitty. She misses you. It's so sad. But it means she really loves you." Amanda says it like she's talking to a child.

Knowing Amanda was in our place opens a dark door. I

take back what I'd said about understanding if Jae-Mee moves on. My heart floods with fear.

"I had to stop in to feed her, and Amanda had to use the bathroom." It's like Jae-Mee read my mind.

"Awkward," Amanda sings to herself.

"Sit down," says Jae-Mee, as a chair to my right squeaks.

He walks around the foot of the bed and plops down in the chair to my left.

"The doctor says there's no change. I still have hope but you know… it's rough. It's been nearly three weeks of no improvement."

"Is it that long already?" says Amanda.

"Yeah. It's crazy. Every day I wake up, I'm surprised her side of the bed is empty. Then I remember."

"That must be so hard for you."

"It sucks." Jae-Mee sighs, bouncing his knee. "But not as bad as it does for Shay. At least I can live my life, mostly. When Shay wakes up, it'll all be lost time to her."

"Your pain matters, too. Don't minimize it." She's right, but hearing her comforting him annoys me.

"I know, I know. I just wish there was something I could do. I'm kind of at a loss." His voice cracks a little.

Amanda rises and shuffles around to his side. "It's okay. Let it out. You can't hold this stuff in. It'll eat away at you."

"I'm fine. Man. Embarrassing…"

"Don't be embarrassed."

"I'm good. Really."

Amanda's sits back down. "If you need anything at all, I'm here for you. The whole KAD community is."

"Thanks."

We sit in silence. Amanda rifles through her bag and unwraps a piece of gum. I listen to the rhythm of her chewing, and it delivers me to my innermost demons.

A chair pushes back with a screech, and I wake to the present.

"I'm sorry, Shay. Next time I'll be in better form. You ready, Amanda?"

"Yep. Bye, Shay. Hope to see you again soon. But, like, better."

At the door, Amanda stops. "Oh shit. Do you mind if we stop back at your place before you drop me home? I think I might have left my keys there."

"Sure, no problem."

I hear their footsteps retreating down the hall.

HOW TOS

I've never had an orgasm sober. When I'm alone, I take it to the edge and drop it just before the big fall. With others, I fake it. I don't want them to feel insecure.

Something about allowing myself that much pleasure feels wrong. I feel guilty. I fear it.

The first time with a guy is the best performance. I aim to be the hottest, most insatiable woman. I do everything they want, trying to surprise them into a serotonin-flooded oblivion. And I'm always drunk or high. Sober sex is the worst. Sober sex is like pita bread pizza. It's a poor substitution.

Sex with Jae-Mee has been hovering in pita bread pizza territory since we started living together. Before that, all I wanted was to be around him all day, every day. But as soon as I could be, things started to change. We no longer met up in restaurants and bars, stumbling home after a night of fun.

He'd approach me in the middle of the day with no mystery, smoke, or mirrors. It's harder to act when I'm so in my head.

He'd open the shower curtain and see me naked in broad daylight—or even worse, under fluorescent lights. It's hard to feel sexy when you're acutely aware that your imperfections are highlighted.

And then the weird shit started.

Jae-Mee deserves better than what I had to offer then—and certainly now. Maybe Amanda will gyrate him back to normalcy. I should be grateful.

With nothing else to do, I make lists in my head.

How to Lose the Man You Thought Would Father Your Children:

- Involuntarily knee him in the nuts whenever he touches you.
- Get weird about physical affection.
- Shut down your womanly wiles.
- Get annoyed when he tries to discuss the sudden lack of sex.
- Accuse him of pressuring you when he lies down beside you.
- Find yourself hospitalized and unresponsive.
- Stay selfishly trapped inside your own head.
- Realize your life is wasting away.
- Roll a hundred miniature clay replicas of yourself into fetal positions in your head.
- Send a wrecking ball through your brain to crush them all.
- Pray that the hospital gets struck by lightning, sending an electrical burst through the equipment attached to you, stopping your heart.

How to Cope When Your Boyfriend Might Be Having Sex with Korean Barbie and You're Catatonic:

- Claw at your imagination for being so visually explicit.
- Remember all the words to Adele's "Rolling in the Deep" and imagine screaming them while roaring recklessly up 95N at night with the windows down.

- Conjure up the photo she posted of herself in a string bikini. Sharpie in sprouting pubic hair and a gruesome disease.
- Construct a dart board from her inflatable body parts.
- Imagine her strutting across the street towards him. As the light turns, she twists her ankle, falls, and gets hit by a Mack Truck.
- Laugh until you cry.
- Scold yourself for being cruel.
- Scold yourself for being catatonic.
- Picture hitting yourself in the head with a blow-up flaccid penis.
- Picture yourself howling with laughter.
- Bemoan how psychotic you've become.
- Envision black paint slowly dripping over every scene until there's nothing left.

PROVOCATION

My brain is spiraling out of control. I can't get visions of Jae-Mee and Korean Barbie out of my head. I will him to come back and tell me I've nothing to fear. And when that doesn't happen, I wish for anyone who can steer me back to land.

"Hello! Remember me? It's Aunt Audrey." One of Mother's friends arrives. Heavy floral perfume floods my nose and I curse myself for wishing so hard.

"Listen honey, I know we've only met once or twice, but I just felt awful about your situation. I was talking with Aileen on the phone and she told me where I could find you."

Audrey drops both hands to my forearm. She takes a quick, deep breath and exhales through her teeth.

"You know honey, I was adopted—from within the US, but I understand how it feels to be you. Now, I don't want to meddle but your mother told me you stopped talking to her before this all happened?"

Audrey pauses and clears her throat—long enough for me to realize she thinks I'm the one who broke off communication.

"My mother is dead now. May God rest her soul. We didn't have the greatest relationship—but I won't bore you with my sob stories. I only mean to say that whatever you think your mother did wrong, you need to let it go. Forgive and forget. Give up this charade already and go pay her a visit. She loves you so much."

Audrey pinches my skin so hard that my own voice echoes around in my head.

"I'm just trying to bring you to your senses. I would've given my right arm to have a mother like yours. All she ever does is talk about how wonderful you kids are doing; how happy she is to have raised you. You all mean the world to her. And it's breaking her heart to have you in here like this."

She lifts my arm and—motherfucking hell—begins tickling my armpit. I've never been a violent girl but I would belt her if I could.

"Us adoptees are a tough breed. Don't I know it. But you know, you've got to grow up someday and stop blaming everything on your parents. You need to take responsibility for your own life. Don't just give up and lay here like this. You hear me? No matter what pain you've been through and what wrongs you think they've done you." Her voice shakes. "Child, I was set on fire by my own father. You don't know the pain I've had to forgive."

I'd wondered about her scars.

"Now, I've seen the photo albums of you kids when you were young. You were smiling and well dressed in every one. I've heard stories about all the awards you've won in school. No troubled kid would excel the way you did. I've known your mother now for two years and that's long enough to understand the kind of person she is."

Audrey squeezes my nose and covers my mouth.

"If she hurt you, I'm sure it was just human error. Mothers are people too, you know. We do everything we can and no matter what we sacrifice and achieve, our children grow up to be our biggest critics. Now, is that the way you want to live? Is this how you want to spend the rest of your life? You're going to waste away some of your best years and the last of your childbearing ones."

This crazy lady's going to kill me.

Her voice sounds further away now—like it's coming from underwater or through a long tunnel. "Shay… Come on, Shay. I know you're in there. I know you hear me and I'm pretty sure you have control enough to do what you need to do. Wake up and let's do this together. It won't be as hard as you think. I'm right here with you."

I begin to wonder if I'm dreaming.

The heart monitor beeps faster. I start coughing. Audrey takes her hands from my face and snaps her fingers next to my ears. "Snap out of it, Shay. Come on, honey."

Footsteps hurry towards my room. "What's going on here? Step out of the way."

Audrey sighs. "She's fine. She's just faking. Can't you people tell?"

"We need you out of the room. Now!"

I'm reminded of how we often stop noticing things until they change. I begin to wonder what shifted in my own life to end up like this.

One thing is clear: Everyone thinks I'm seeking attention to make Mother look bad. They believe I have control. The thing is: I never have.

But like it or not, I'm no longer maintaining the status quo.

HIDING IN PLAIN SIGHT

I'm floating in the middle of the ocean in my brain. I want to jump out of this flimsy yellow raft, but I can't seem to move. I'm a spirit trapped inside a dead body, haunting myself insane.

They say the best way to hide is in plain sight.

I disguised my Asianness behind my white family. I hid my poverty behind their bounty. I tucked my loneliness under a smile. I buried the woman who bore me somewhere inside my mother where I could never quite reach her.

If someone were to open me up, they'd find parts of me missing. I may have rejected a wholeness of body in the same way I've rejected the idea that somewhere, there might live another mother who either lost me or let me go.

And so I'm hiding again in plain sight.

I rock my brain to sleep with hollow sentiments. It's just a bad day—we all have them. Tomorrow's another chance. I recite all the clichés and platitudes that can help one eke by when they just need something to hang their heart on.

It's just me in my flimsy yellow raft, unable to drop anchor. I float aimlessly, praying for land.

OLD FAITHFUL

I'm knocked back to my childhood again.

I woke to the clock in the living room ticking, its sound traveling all the way down the hall to my bed and tapping my ear drums awake. I couldn't get it to stop. Its relentlessness was unnerving.

Tick tick tick tick tick tick tick.

Rolling onto my right, I lifted my knees to my chest.

Myra's muffled voice called out in the night. She must've been in high school around then. I was just finishing up the fifth grade.

Tick tick tick tick tick tick tick.

I slid further under the covers and rolled to my left, sticking my head under the pillow. I closed my eyes tightly, trying to imagine another sound—any sound—to drown out Myra and all that damn ticking.

Tick tick tick tick tick.

My eyes popped open, the darkness resolving into shapes and color.

My closet door was ajar. I couldn't sleep when it was open. I told myself that I noticed it earlier and forgot, so my brain must've woken me to close it.

Sitting on the edge of the bed, I let the room settle from its spin. I felt like one of the particles trapped in a snow globe. I tested one foot on the floor, and then the other. I walked across the room and slid the closet door shut. It echoed like a distant drum.

Myra's voice was a little softer when she groaned.

I wanted to tell her, "Wake up, big sister. It's just a bad dream. Remember? I have them, too."

But I knew it was pointless. When those nightmares visited me, I just lay there waiting for them to end.

Be brave, Myra. Be brave.

I pressed my ear to the door—like listening to the waves in a seashell, controlled by the man in the moon.

Tick tick tick.

It never stopped.

Some hearts must be stronger than others.

Tick.

I twisted the knob on my bedroom door and poked my head out into the darkness. I peered down the hall, squinting my eyes to adjust them.

I tiptoed down the hall. When the floor creaked below me, I marveled at how quiet it kept during regular waking hours. Perhaps it had something to tell me?

For one unsteady moment, I stood outside Myra's room, listening to her toss and turn. I carefully continued on, making my way past the kitchen to the parlor—the pivotal room before my parents' wing.

The clock was thundering in my ears.

TICK. TICK. TICK.

I imagined all the parts of the house came alive in the dark, like a clowder of alley cats eager to tell me the tales of their lives.

I watched the blue feathers in the etched vase as they danced in the moonlight.

TICK TICK TICK TICK TICK.

I quietly clicked my tongue to the beat of the second hand, to harness my nervous energy.

I snickered a little, picturing my old piano teacher with his metronome and his broken black-rimmed glasses. He used white tape to hold them together in the middle—like a cartoon nerd.

My focus returned to the hallway and its chattering floorboards. I sharpened my ear. The creaking wasn't very rhythmic—not like the old faithful clock.

Not everything that makes sound is music, my piano teacher would say.

Myra was still crying. I thought again about waking her.

The hallway creaked—nearer, and then farther away. I lay still, goosebumps popping out on my forearms and legs—oh so still, so the man in the moon wouldn't see me.

After fifteen more ticks, I crept back to my room, my heart racing.

Tick tick tick.

I clicked along with my tongue until I fell back to sleep.

THE SIREN

I hear people running through hallways. The pulsing shriek explodes disco lights in my head.

"We need to evacuate. Move everyone out!" a woman shouts.

Someone rushes into my room. They're disconnecting and reconnecting things, and then I'm gliding feet-first through the hall.

I'd forgotten what it's like to be mobile. It's like a theme park ride through a dark haunted house. I sense the lights shifting in brightness and hue.

It's dizzying chaos after static solitude. I feel more alive than I have since my arrival.

"Andy! You can't take the elevator, man! They need to be carried!"

"Shit," the voice above my head—Andy—says.

I think I'm shoved into a room. My bed rolls to a stop. A door closes. It feels dark in here.

The siren is louder than ever. Sirens from outside blend into the panicked symphony.

Not everything that makes sound is music, I say in my head. And then I think how not every sound has to be music. It can still serve a purpose.

But the musical side of my brain tries to restructure the

wild repetition. I'm dancing slowly under candy-colored lights at a rave in my head. And the drugs never felt so good. Something must've changed in transition.

Ooh-eee! Ooh-eee! Ooh-eee! Err! Err!

Ooh-eee! Ooh-eee! Ooh-eee! Err! Err!

The sound vibrates through my skin. Everything starts to bend. My mind. My heart. My body. It all feels like vibrantly colored oil slowly dripping between two sheets of glass.

Suddenly, I'm a bird soaring through kaleidoscope skies.

I wonder why life can't always feel like this.

Everything that goes up must come down. It's just balance and science and shit. Get out of your mind. Let yourself go with the flow like you did when you were young.

Let yourself be. You're along for the ride. It feels good. Doesn't it? It feels good when you don't question things. Life is simpler this way. Don't you see? Life doesn't have to be hard.

Give yourself to the moment. That's a good girl. You're doing great. You're my little girl. Aren't you? God doesn't let things happen unless they should. Everything happens for a reason. That's why you're here. That's why you're with me.

Something shifts.

I can't hear the sirens anymore and wonder when they stopped.

Who was that? Who are you? What were you saying?

Oh, nothing. Just go back to sleep. You'll forget about it all in the morning.

The buzz in my blood dissipates. The quiet envelops me.

I suddenly wonder where I am and where everyone else is. Did that man—Andy—did he take me downstairs? Or am I still in the darkened room? Has the building burned down with me in it? Am I dead or alive?

You're doing it again.

A giant foam finger slowly wags in my head.

Hush now. Just look at the clock's second hand. Let it lull you safely back to sleep.

HELLO?

I don't know who I am. I am often not me.

I open my eyes to a large, rocky cave. Small children in blindfolds hold handmade knives. They wander around with their arms outstretched, hoping to find me.

There's a woman. She's mute. She sits high in the center watching over us.

I want to say, I don't know where I am. You must have the wrong girl. But I can't speak.

The woman starts to hum. She communicates on another frequency. She doesn't need to use words for her children to understand.

They're coming towards me.

I creep back until I hit the jagged brown stone, trying not to make a sound. But the rocks beneath me aren't sturdy. Fragments crack and roll away.

The woman hums at a higher pitch. Its vibrations crumble more rocks, clearing a path for the children.

I don't want to believe the kids would hurt me. They're beautiful children. But there are so many of them and just one of whoever I am. And the woman seems to have such a powerful, unspoken control.

As they near, I close my eyes tightly. Tighter. So tight that it hurts.

I think: You can't stay here, Shay. Use your powers. You've got to find a way out of here or you'll die. Save yourself.

With my eyes closed so tight I can feel the blood rushing to my face, I imagine I'm out of the cave. I picture green grass with the sun beating down on it. I see dandelion wishes ready to be blown. I bend to grab one. I press my lips together and push the breath out of my mouth. The feathery seeds dance in the air. I hear the laughter of a little girl.

I step sideways from the blinded children, recoiling from their weapons.

Think harder! Try harder!

Little daggers stab shallowly into my stomach. It hurts like hell.

"Stay with me!" someone in my head shouts.

I squeeze my eyes tighter. And then I open them to blackness. I'm not sure if I'm still dreaming or if the dream flipped.

Little daggers continue to stab at my stomach.

I hear people moving around outside.

I try to say hello, and think that I do, but it's hard to know what's real.

I lift up my head and the dark fades to a lighter shade of black. My body's stretched out before me under a tiny patterned sheet. I watch as I turn my left foot side to side, then my right.

"Hello?" I try, louder. "Hello? Hello?"

I'm pretty sure I'm me now. But am I awake? Am I real?

I push down on my elbows and lift myself up just a bit before crashing back down.

I scream at the top of my lungs, "Hello? Hello?"

The door opens and piercing light hits my eyes. I recoil.

"Hello?" says a voice. "What… the hell?"

"Hello?" I whisper. "Are you there? Or am I still dreaming?"

GODDAMN MIRACLE

Being awake is overwhelming. I long to fade back into the background. My inner self tries to escape my body, but I stop her. Not so fast. Not this time.

"Twenty-three days," says a familiar voice. "Welcome back, Miss Stone. Nice to finally meet you."

I feel drunk. It's hard to get the words out. "Yeah. Same."

"Three weeks and change," he informs me, with a smirk. "That's quite the cat nap." His face looks like it's in high definition. Everything seems too real. "Do you remember what happened?"

Glancing up at the lights, I search my mind. "Well, I woke up in a dark room."

"I'm sorry, I meant before that—before you got here."

"My boyfriend came home from work. I couldn't speak or move."

"No memories of what might have caused your perceived paralysis?"

"No." I ruminate on the word Perceived.

"Okay. Well, you're here now and that's what matters. Maybe it'll come to you later. And if it doesn't? That's okay, too. Everyone loves a good mystery." He winks.

I want to say it's not so great when that mystery is your life.

"Could you hear us? Could you feel us moving you around?"

"Yes." I wiggle my fingers, marveling at the sensation. "I heard and felt everything. But after a while, things got blurred. It was hard to tell what was real and what I was imagining."

He nods as if he's satisfied with my words, but I can tell he wants more. "Someone will call your family and partner. We'll need to run a few tests, but you can see them as soon as tomorrow afternoon."

This is supposed to be good news. But I'm not ready. I attempt a smile while panic sets in.

An hour later, the physical therapist props me up in a chair, manipulating my limbs with great care. "It's a miracle," she tells me. "Someone was watching over you, girl."

She has me bend and straighten things on my own, twisting from the waist and neck.

"You're pretty lucky, you know. You'll tire out easier while you build your strength back. You can expect nine to twelve weeks of regular PT. And you'll need a chair for a while—mostly as a precaution. But damn, girl." She shakes her head. "I've been moving you around every day, trying not to lose hope. You were nothing but dead weight."

"I knew it was you."

"Why? Do I smell?"

"Everyone has a scent. It's not bad. But I must."

"Naw. We took care of you. And—like a lot of lucky East Asians, you don't have bad BO. My sister-in-law's Korean and told me something about a missing gene that keeps your bacteria from eating itself. Sounds gross, but that's what causes the smell on the rest of us."

"Huh," I grunt. "Who knew? Guess all that deodorant was for nothing."

"Right?" She laughs. "Now you know."

"What's your name?"

"Lakeisha."

"Thanks, Lakeisha."

"What for?" She's crouched down, rolling my ankles.

"Everything. And not treating me like I'm some sort of psychopath. I overheard some of the others…"

"Well, it's my job. And don't mind the others. No one understands catatonia. I think they're afraid of it. Yours was especially rare—kind of like dying without being dead. But I knew you were in there."

"How?"

Twisting my wrists, she fixes her eyes on mine. "I could feel you in there."

"I don't believe in God. At least not in that way."

"That's okay. He believes in you."

I decide not to get into it. I can see that it helps her. But I'll never be the God Only Gives What You Can Take kind of girl.

"I do believe in the energy of life. Whatever you want to call that."

"It's okay. I'm not here to convert you. I'm just trying to help you get back on your feet. Speaking of which, can you hold onto these poles?"

I grab the parallel bars and Lakeisha guides me to stand.

I chuckle. "It's like doing gymnastics in PE."

"Well, don't do anything crazy. Unless you want to break something and stay here longer."

"As tempting as that sounds, no, thanks."

"Take it easy." She clutches me under my arms.

"Stop tickling," I groan, wriggling around.

"You know, some things were easier when you were dead

weight."

"Maybe for you."

She steps back. "You know what, Miss Stone?"

I mimic her head tilt. "What's that, Lakeisha?"

"You're going to be alright. It's a Goddamn miracle. I don't care what you say."

RETURN

Jae-Mee rushes in. I see him with my own eyes, not just in memory. With my nose to his neck, I inhale the sweet vanilla in his hair and the natural musk of his skin. When he squeezes me tight, I briefly lose sensation in my limbs and nearly panic. He backs up, shakes his head, and says, "Holy shit. I can hardly believe it."

"I'm so sorry," I begin, then burst into tears. I've never been a crier, but these tears are determined to roll out.

He pulls me close again and declares, "You have nothing to be sorry for."

But I know that's not true. "I've put you through so much."

"Aw, babe... Don't worry about me. You're the one who's been stuck here."

"Not just while I've been here."

He studies my face. "What are you talking about? You didn't put me through anything. God, I've missed you so much."

"I was a bad girlfriend."

"You were not." He embraces me again.

"I want you to know, I understand if... if you had to find comfort in someone else."

His eyes roll to the ceiling for a moment. "They said you

might be confused. And that we'd need to take it one day at a time."

"I mean Amanda."

His body relaxes. "Is that what this is about? You could hear our visit?" I nod. He shakes his head. "She begged me to bring her. And you thought something happened between us?"

"Maybe? Well, yes."

He laughs. "Never gonna happen."

"Mother always said I have an overactive imagination. Have you talked to her?"

"She wouldn't speak to me directly. I had to go through Myra."

"I don't think she ever visited."

Jae-Mee shrugs, sympathetically. "Might've been too hard to see you that way. I wanted to come more—and I should've—but seeing you was rough. If I'd known you were aware, I'd have been here every day."

"It's okay. I needed time to think."

"Any big revelations?"

"Just a lot of dwelling on the past and watching my mind unravel."

"Sounds like you needed less time to think!"

I smile at him. "This right here is a gift. Being alive and awake here with you."

As he holds me, my hands sweep over his shoulders and back. I'm filled with gratitude for being able to feel him. I clutch his face with both hands. "You look better than I remembered."

Recoiling, he quips, "You could use a little mouthwash."

I cover my mouth, horrified.

He laughs. "It's nice to see the life back in you. Doc says

you can come home in a week."

"Home," I repeat, letting the word rattle around on my tongue.

"I talked to the landlord. She's hiring someone to set up the ramp. A little PT and you'll be back to your old self in no time."

"Seems too good to be true. Can I really just go home to my old life? What will I do? When will I go back to work? Do I even still have a job?"

"We'll figure it all out together. Try not to worry about it now. Just focus on getting well enough to come home."

TOLERANCE AND RESILIENCE

I savor each spoonful of real food, letting it sit on my tongue. It's nothing exciting—mashed fruit or an assortment of mushy beans and rice. But it all tastes like hope.

I'm transferred to the rehab wing where the more able-bodied patients reside. I have my own television and a decent view of the park. After flipping through hundreds of mind-numbing channels, I choose the park.

Staring out at the functioning world is the antithesis of being trapped inside my own mind. There are birds and squirrels and street cats and dogs. There are kids on skateboards, business people on phones, and mothers pushing strollers. I contemplate what my future holds and what my body might be capable of once I'm out.

When Lakeisha wheels me to therapy, I ask, "How bad was the fire?"

"Fire? What fire?"

"Wasn't there a fire? I remember the sirens…" I panic, fearing it's more proof of my unreliable mind.

"Oh, that wasn't a fire. There was a man running around with a gun trying to get revenge on a surgeon. That's probably what you heard."

I'm oddly relieved. "Is that how I ended up in the closet?"

"I don't know about that. You'll have to speak to someone

else."

"Was there someone named Andy?"

She gasps. "Wow, you really were in there. Andy got shot in the leg. He's pretty traumatized by the whole thing."

"He was shot by the gunman?"

"No, a security guard. He was mistaken for the shooter."

"Shit…"

"It's a hot mess," she grumbles. "The shooter was white. Andy's black."

"Oh… Did they catch him—the shooter?"

"Yeah, they got him."

"Maybe Andy saved my life by shoving me in that closet. How long after that was I found?"

"Twenty-something hours, but don't quote me. I don't want to cause any trouble."

I tell Lakeisha my theory of how awareness stems from some kind of change.

"It's funny how I stopped hearing the heart monitor until my heart raced and the tempo sped up. It was there all along, right beside my head. But it took a change in tempo to remember it was there."

"And sometimes we don't realize how much we love someone till they're gone," Lakeisha adds.

"True. Why does it have to be like that?"

"Everything happens for a reason," she recites, to my horror. "The Lord works in mysterious ways."

I bite my tongue.

In our session, I learn that while I still have a decent range of muscle and movement, I can't manage much for long.

"You just need to build up your tolerance and resilience," she tells me, as if it's no big deal.

"Story of my life."

NONSENSE

Myra's heels click down the hall with unmistakable determination. I sit in my wheelchair facing the park, contemplating how I'll respond to the family. I can't know for sure if the scenes I remembered were real.

"Shay!" She trots over to squeeze me, planting a big sticky kiss on my cheek. "You did it! I knew you could!" She flips her hair from her face, the way Mother does. Although she's changed her looks quite a bit, she's still so much like her.

I smile as naturally as I can.

"I would've been here sooner but you know—life is busy out there! I was here three times a week though."

"You were?"

"Do you think I'd let my sister rot in here on her own?"

My heart races. I try to stay calm. "It's just that I don't remember it that way."

"Don't worry. It's not your fault," she assures, playing with my hair. "It must've been so confusing for you."

I just nod in response.

"So! I bet you're wondering what's going on with everyone." Myra sits on the bed, lifting her feet to admire her shiny new shoes. "Let's see… Mother and Daddy are so happy you're awake. Your party is going to be epic. Ivan and Tamara are pregnant again and Andrei just keeps getting cuter! Jack's been with the same girl a few weeks now. That's a record for him. And Graham's practically famous."

"That's great," I say, feeling tired already.

"You know what? I'm going to book you an appointment with my guy to fix up this hair. It's on me. You'll look great for the party."

"I'm going to be limited for a while with what I can do," I explain, gathering my hair to one side.

"I'll bring him to you," she says, smiling. "Anything for my little sis."

"Thanks. The party, though—can we skip it? It's gonna take a while to get back to full speed. At least a few months."

"Nonsense!" Myra coos. "It's already in the works. Don't let Mother down. She's throwing everything into it. She's so excited about your recovery."

"My recovery is just beginning. Can we keep it small then? Immediate family only? I don't have the energy for crowds."

Myra frowns. "Everyone will understand if you get a little sleepy. They just want to see you! They've been asking about you nonstop."

"It's not like I've been off traveling the world," I grumble.

"Don't be like that. It's awkward for people. It was hard enough for me. No one knows what to say or do… Besides, some probably came and you just don't remember."

"I remember."

"Oh yeah?" Myra's eyes narrow as her head tilts. "Then what happened, Shay? How'd you end up here in the first place?"

"That I don't know."

"You see?" she says, satisfied. "Your memory's unreliable. You don't even remember I was here all those times. All that effort for what?"

"Sorry. Maybe you're right."

"I don't mean to give you a hard time, Shay. Just don't give anyone else one. Trust me. People have been doing their best trying to make sense of your being in here."

"Yeah, I know."

"On my way out, I'll get one of the nurses to bring you some magazines. Pick something cute. I'll arrange for Tommy to come by. I'll pay him double if I have to. I don't care."

"Do I really look that bad?"

Myra examines me with pursed lips. "Yeah, but anyone would after lying in bed for that long."

She laughs and I join her. In a way, I'm comforted by the familiarity of it all.

"That's the Shay I know and love!" She gives me a quick squeeze. "Listen, I've got to run. See you next week!"

I nearly go deaf from her kiss.

FRESH START

I used to daydream about starting over. On many walks through the neighborhood, I'd imagine what it'd be like if I could just hit rewind.

Maybe if I were an easier child, things would've been different. Perhaps if I were more agreeable and asked fewer questions, I'd have gotten the love that I craved.

While I can't go back in time, I've been granted the opportunity to start again. Maybe I should let everyone else start over, too.

Maybe Lakeisha and millions of others are right and everything does happen for a reason.

I just wish I could get some solid answers. How much of what flowed through my mind was the truth? How much was the drugs? And how much is just further proof of what Mother and Myra say is my faulty brain?

I have many reasons to be grateful: I've miraculously woken from over three weeks of catatonia. My body seems to be functioning well. The love of my life is taking me back. My sister is treating me with kindness and says the rest of the family awaits my return. It would be just like the old me to gloss over all that joy and focus on minor grievances.

When Tommy struts into my room, I tell him I want a shaggy bob. And I'd like a purple balayage if he can manage it, but he tells me the color will have to wait.

He winces, combing through my limp locks with a face like he's navigating a minefield. "Myra warned it would be a project. But don't worry. We'll survive this together."

For the past few years I've been cutting my own hair. I thought I was getting by. But when Tommy's done with me, I see just what a real haircut can do.

"Wow," I say to the girl in the mirror.

"I know," Tommy sighs, admiring his work. "I would never have believed it myself."

When Jae-Mee walks in, he does a double-take. "You look amazing!"

"It was a gift from Myra."

He leans in to kiss me and asks, "Already making deals with the devil?"

"Is that what you think of her?"

"Well, she's not a nice person—at least not to me, and I don't like how she treats you. But I know she's your family, so…"

"I had a lot of dreams—or memories—of Myra and the rest of the family. They've kind of left me reeling. I'm trying to figure out how much is true."

"Do they feel true?"

I shrug, adding, "Some do. But, you know—I was medicated. And catatonic. That doesn't make me the best judge of things. I think maybe to find out, I need to start fresh with everyone. See how it plays out in real-time."

"Okay. How was PT?"

"Great. Lakeisha says I'll make a full recovery in three-to-four months."

Jae-Mee squeezes my knee. I grin.

"Maybe I can do better this time."

"With what?"

"The way I deal with people, my feelings... You know. Everything."

"Okay," he says, nodding. "We could all be better at those things—myself included."

I put my hand on top of his. It's these little expressions of affection that I missed the most.

"But, sometimes," he continues, "it's not all up to you. I just don't want you to think it's your fault if you give it your best and things still go sour. Both sides have to put in the effort for things to get better. At least that's what omma always says."

"Of course," I say, wishing I had someone to call omma.

"But I'm glad you're hopeful. It's a good way to be. Now, let's get you home!"

As Jae-Mee wheels me towards the ramp of our building, my heart feels like a jumping bean. It's hard to believe I've been gone a whole month—and am actually returning.

I'm barely through the door before Paisley leaps onto my lap. Her purr is so loud and her fur is so silky. She performs clumsy somersaults across my thighs.

"Show off. I've missed you, too." I lift her to my face and inhale her scruff.

As Jae-Mee wheels me through the living room, something feels off. He must sense my hesitation. "What's wrong?"

"Nothing," I say, not wanting to bring him down. "It's just crazy being back home again."

"Do you remember when I came home and found you?" He sits down and pulls me near.

Nodding, I say, "It was awful. You walked in and I wanted to say 'hi.' That's when I realized I couldn't speak. I tried to sit up but I couldn't move. It was like one of those nightmares when you can't run or scream."

"I was so fucking scared," he confesses. "I looked around for pills... Thought you might have taken something..."

"I hated that I couldn't tell you—not that I'd have known what to say."

"Fuck, that was bad. What about before I came home? Do you remember any of that?"

"That's what everyone wants to know. But, nothing. When you walked in, it was like I woke up inside myself but my body was still sleeping."

"Are you going back to Dottie?"

"I don't know..."

"You've gotta see someone. They said—"

"Yeah, I know." I visualize Dottie and my skin crawls. "I'm still a little resentful."

"She meant well. Didn't she?"

Thinking back on my memories, I shrug. "Who knows? Maybe she was right to badger me about Mother."

"Are you going to call her? Your mother?"

Wheeling the chair back and forth, I ask, "Do you think I should?"

"What I think doesn't matter. You know her best."

I sigh. "I should call her. Maybe it's childish of me but I wish she'd be the one to call."

"She should. But you know that she won't. So instead of hoping she'll be the person you wish she was, maybe you should just try to accept that this is who she is."

Somewhere in a closet in my mind, a voice screams so loudly it echoes through my skull. But I ignore it and smile. "That's a good idea. You're wicked smaht, dude."

GOALS

Dottie holds the door open as Jae-Mee wheels me into the familiar room. The white porcelain cat still rests on the third shelf. The Aztec-printed blanket still drapes across the back of the beige couch. And Dottie still wears gold-rimmed glasses and light-colored slacks. The only difference is a faint scent of lavender in the air that I hadn't noticed before.

Jae-Mee says, "I'll be back in forty-five," before a quick kiss goodbye.

Dottie shuts the door and makes her way to her chair. "Well," she begins, "I'm glad to see you."

"It's not my decision," I inform her, gliding to a stop by the couch. "The hospital wouldn't release me without therapy and I didn't want to start over."

She smiles, unaffected. "Okay. I appreciate your honesty. What do you want to talk about?"

"Where do I start? It's so overwhelming." I pause. "I've had so much time to think about everything—things I've either forgotten on purpose or by mistake. Or maybe weren't real to begin with." I sigh. "I'm probably not making sense."

"Go on." She nods.

"I just want to know what's true. I want to know what to believe in for once."

"What are you so unsure of?"

I huff. "Everything. The circumstances around my birth and adoption. My history with the Stones. Whether I remember things right or if I'm just a crazy, confused girl who doesn't know up from down."

"Well, it's a lot to sort through. But that's what we're here for."

"But I need to know now. At least the things involving my family." Dottie sits calmly, switching the cross of her legs. I continue, "Maybe you were right. I don't know."

"About what?"

"I was mad that you kept trying to get me to talk about Mother. I'd never have sent her that email if it weren't for your questioning. I thought my problems all stemmed from the loss of my first mother. But maybe there's something more…"

"Such as?"

"Just the way she's always doubting my memories and minimizing my feelings. She and Myra both do the same thing. I love them, but… it's to the point where I don't know who to trust. Myra's telling me she came to visit three times a week. I don't even recall three times in total. But, like, I was catatonic so why should I be trusted? I don't even know how I ended up there."

"What can you tell me about the day you fell into catatonia?"

"Very little," I sigh. "It's the million dollar question."

"Do you recall how you were feeling? Were you happy or sad? Did you do anything out of the ordinary?"

"I literally remember nothing. I heard Jae-Mee come home but that was it. I was paralyzed."

"That must've been awfully scary."

"Yeah. Frustrating, to say the least."

"And the rest of your family—have you seen them?"

I shake my head. "They're throwing me a party this weekend."

"How are you feeling about the party?"

"Anxious and I wish I could skip it. But it's nice that they're making the effort. And Myra treated me to this haircut. She sent her stylist into the hospital."

"That was thoughtful."

"See? This is what I mean. They do these generous things—like the haircut and the party. It makes me feel guilty to even think bad thoughts about them."

Dottie says, "You want to find your own truth while staying compassionate to them."

I think for a moment. "Yes. That's what I want."

"Well, let's give it a go, then."

THINGS PEOPLE WRITE

Myra wasn't kidding when she said she tried hacking my accounts. I have to reset all of my passwords. Once I'm able to log in, I'm overwhelmed with notifications. I skip them and jump straight to my wall.

Things People Write on Your Facebook Timeline While You're Hospitalized:

- Hard times make you stronger. Just you wait and see!
- Don't worry. God is never blind to your tears, never deaf to your prayers, and never silent to your pain. He sees, He hears, and He will deliver!
- My beautiful daughter… I miss you so much. We're all rooting for you. You've always been a strong soul. There's no doubt in my mind that if anyone can get through this, it's you. Xx
- You are more than your circumstances.
- When I is replaced with We, even Illness becomes Wellness. We've got your back, Shay! Praying for you!
- Even the darkest night will end and the sun will rise. — Victor Hugo
- If I had a flower for every time I think of you, I'd walk forever in my garden.
- You need a nutritionist, not a hospital. Illness can't live

in an alkalized body.

- You've always been one of my favorite people. I wish I told you more often.
- To all of Shay's friends: My sister can feel the love you're sending her way. I see her every day and know that it's only a matter of time before she's back better than ever. Keep praying! It helps our family to know how loved she is. xoxo
- Damn, Shay. I've always had a crush on you. Get better so I can finally ask you out. (No offense, Shay's boyfriend.)
- S is for Super. H is for Hawtness. A is for Asian. Y is for not finished Yet.
- My aunt was in that hospital last year. The doctors and staff there are aces. You're in good hands!
- Can somebody explain to us what's going on?
- Sending virtual hugs and kisses from Minnesota!
- My poor baby! I'll never forget the first time you looked into my eyes the day we picked you up at the airport. They were sad and scared, like you must feel now. I'd give anything to get you out of there! We love you! Xx
- I don't blame you, Shay. Sometimes I need a break from this world, too.
- You never know how strong you are until strong is the only option.
- I've been meditating for you every day! Sending healing powers!
- I can tell how much your family loves you—and we love you, too!
- Psalm 41:3 The Lord sustains her on her sickbed; in her illness you restore her to full health.
- I believe in you, Shay!

- Hang in there! I'm not ready to lose you!
- Everything will be okay in the end. If it's not okay, then it's not the end.

THE BIG EVENT

No one picks up on the first two tries, but the third time, Myra answers. "Mother says she'll speak to you at the party. She doesn't want to taint the reunion with a cheap phone call."

And so I wait some more.

There's nowhere to park in the old neighborhood. The first open spot is blocks away, leaving Jae-Mee to push my chair half a mile up a steady incline.

"Hope they don't mind that we're late."

"They can't possibly give us a hard time today," I say, with wishful thinking.

My heart races as my eyes trace the trail of cars lining the otherwise quiet neighborhood. As we enter the cul-de-sac, music and voices echo off neutral-colored houses. Someone peers around the corner of the garage and runs away shouting, "She's here!"

I glance up at Jae-Mee. "Don't imagine you feel like running us back to the car?"

He snickers. "Just say when."

A part of me wanted a lie from him, insistence that it'll be fun. But the rest of me needs to hear that twinge of pain in his voice.

Jae-Mee wheels me past the garage to the yard and the crowd screams, "Welcome home!" as I roll in. In the sea of smiling faces, I can't place one.

Music blasts through the speakers: Here she comes just a walkin' down the street, singing do-wah-diddy-diddy-dum-diddy-do.

I'm in a wheelchair. And I hate that song.

I smile awkwardly, scanning the crowd for my family. And, dramatically, the crowd parts as the Stones work their way through, pausing under a floral archway. Cell phones snap photos from every direction. It all seems choreographed—down to who stands where.

"There she is," speaks Mother, clasping her hands in front of her chest. "My baby." She flashes that winning smile, wearing an eggplant-toned dress that sets off her coloring perfectly. "You look beautiful! It's great to see the life back in your cheeks. You looked terrible in the hospital."

"You were there?" I gasp. My brows are furrowing furiously as I try to recall the moment—the one I'd tried not to wait for each day.

"Of course I was." She approaches to give me a big, showy hug. "But I'm so glad you're out of there now."

Father pats me on the shoulder and says, "Welcome back." Ivan follows his lead with a solid whack on the arm, like he's greeting a burly pal. His wife Tamara leans down and kisses my cheek, telling their son Andrei to say hi to Auntie. Jack gives me a careful hug, as if he's afraid he might break me.

Flashes go off all around us and I spot a massive film crew. "What's all this?"

Mother brushes off my question. "Just a little feature for the local news. You won't even know they're here."

Before I can protest, people are bombarding me with hugs and wet kisses. I don't recognize most of them.

"Welcome back!"

"It's good to see you home!"

"It's a miracle!"

After forty-five minutes of intense discomfort, Jae-Mee finds his way back to me. I shoo him away, begging him to either get me a drink or help me escape.

Attractive women in tuxedos work the crowd with hors d'oeuvres. "Prawns? Swedish meatballs?"

"No thanks," I say. "Do you have anything vegetarian?"

"I don't think so but I'll check," one promises, never to return.

Wheeling away from the madness, I observe the entire scene. It's my party but I feel like a sports team mascot. People rest their hands on my shoulder with drive-by positivity, scurrying off before a conversation can start. I feel acknowledged but unseen. In many ways, it's not much different from how things were when I was out cold.

But since I promised myself I'd be optimistic, I keep trying to shove it all out of my mind. I brush away questions of why it seems my family's avoiding me.

Jae-Mee returns with our drinks. "Sorry it took me so long. This place is insane."

I chug half of my drink in one go. "Have you seen my family?"

"They're talking to the press."

"Oh," I groan. "Who are all these people?"

"I was going to ask you."

"I'm exhausted already. Do you think it'd be rude to sneak off without saying goodbye?"

"I'll leave that to you."

"Just the thought of getting through the crowd in this chair..." I begin. "They went through all of this trouble to put up leveled platforms. They look great but I don't want to make a scene trying to maneuver around them."

"Yeah, not the best planning when the guest of honor's in a wheelchair."

"Let's see if we can head out without causing a fuss. I'll text Myra later."

THE CASE

Art Starr sends flowers and a bottle of expensive sparkling wine. He calls to personally welcome me back to the waking world. And he offers an opportunity to work from home fifteen hours a week at a higher rate, to make up some of the difference. "Just consider your month off a paid vacation," he jokes. I want to say, "Some vacation," but he ends the call before I get a chance.

The door buzzer screeches. I wheel my way to the intercom but can't quite reach. Hoisting myself off the arms of the chair, it slides out from beneath me and I crash to the floor.

The buzzer wails three more times.

I struggle on my way back up, slapping the damn button that unlocks the door. Lowering myself back into the chair, I roll towards the door as someone knocks.

"It's me!" shouts Myra.

"Coming," I holler, hoping to incite a little patience.

When I open the door, Myra says, "You're sweating! Did I interrupt anything?" She peers around as if hoping to catch a glimpse of something scandalous.

"I fell trying to reach the intercom."

"Clumsy," she jests, pecking me on the cheek. "Did you enjoy the party?"

"It was great." I try to sound convincing.

"Good. It was a bitch to organize. You have no idea."

"I bet."

Myra opens the fridge, cracks open a fizzy water, and sits herself down on the couch.

"This is where he found you. Isn't it?" Her eyes scan left to right. I nod. She asks, "You really don't remember anything at all?"

"Just what I already said," I tell her, trying to feign patience.

"Well, memory has never been your strong suit." I freeze for a moment. "But that's not what I'm here to talk about. Let me cut to the chase. How long were you in that closet before they found you?"

"About a day. Why?"

"I thought so." She beams, sitting taller and brighter. "I was talking to Mother and we think we have a pretty strong case."

"Against who? For what?"

Myra rolls her eyes. "The hospital. They were grossly negligent. If you hadn't woken and caught their attention, you could've died."

"But I didn't. And I might not have woken at all if things didn't happen like they did. I could still be in a coma—or whatever—catatonia."

"Oh Shay." Myra shakes her head. "You lost a month of life. And you'll be like this for God knows how long. Don't you want something to show for that?"

"No. It's not anyone's fault."

"I'm not saying it is. But you could've died in their care. You should be compensated for that."

"I'm doing okay. My company paid my time off and I still

have a job. Honestly, I'm just happy to be alive."

"Oh, sweetie," she says, giving me puppy dog eyes. "And we're thrilled for that, too. But they shouldn't be able to get away with what happened. We need to make them care enough so it never happens again. You know—they didn't even call to tell us you were missing. They probably didn't even know."

"What could you have done?"

"Let me make myself clear," Myra says, taking a swig from the can and slamming it down. "We don't need to include you in the process. We can do it without you."

I'm suddenly reminded of that time I got my credit report and learned they opened three accounts in my name for some reason that failed to make sense.

"Why would you do that? Don't you have tons of money?"

"No, we don't have tons of money. Jesus! And that party didn't pay for itself. Everyone's just trying to scrape by. We all have expenses."

"You are? You do? I thought you'd have stashed mountains of money away by now. What about your modeling careers and living at home?"

"Don't be so naive. God! You've always asked too many questions."

I take a moment to respond. "Maybe I have."

"Thank you!" Myra chugs the last of the can.

"It's just that I feel kind of bad about it. They took good care of me in there—aside from that one thing that ended up being a good thing."

"Okay," Myra declares, rising to leave. "We'll keep you out of it then."

IT AIN'T RIGHT

After learning about my spill, Jae-Mee rigs up a wooden stick duct-taped to the buzzer. I don't mention the bit about my family's plans to sue the hospital. I'm probably too optimistic—or as Myra says, naive—hoping they'll just let it go.

Paisley makes it her mission to ensure I don't disappear again, monitoring my every move. I put on some Lana Del Rey, and with Paisley on my lap, I dance us around in my chair, singing, "Ever since my baby went away…"

We roll backwards, forwards, and slowly spin counter-clockwise. Her little round face squints up at me and I smile, carrying on. We move through the shadows and sunbeams together. It's like a David Lynch disco in slow motion.

God, it feels good to be alive.

When the buzzer sounds, I roll us over to the wall to let in Lakeisha. She doesn't typically work off-site, but she and the hospital agreed to make special provisions for me twice a week.

"Look at you, Miss Thang," she says, letting herself in the unlocked door. "Hi cat."

Paisley scampers off to her safe place under the couch.

"Have you been doing the exercises I taught you every day?"

"Yes, ma'am."

"Good. Then I'm going to sit my ass down and watch you go through each one."

"Grab yourself something to drink," I offer, nodding towards the kitchen.

"I'm good."

I wheel myself over to the walker and begin my first set of movements.

Lakeisha chatters on. "Nice piece on the news the other night. I assume my invitation got lost in the mail."

"Oh, the party? Sorry. I had no say in it. I hardly knew anyone there. It was a circus."

"Your mother's beautiful."

"Yep, she is. Have you seen her before—at the hospital?"

"Nope. I've only seen your sister, before she got banned." She snickers.

"That really happened?"

"Yes, indeed. She's a tough cookie."

"Yes, indeed," I echo. "You know, Myra's trying to tell me she was there three times a week. She says my memory is faulty. She doesn't realize my brain was awake all along."

"Why would she lie about something like that?"

"I guess 'cause she thinks it makes her look good. She told my friends she was there every day. My family's peculiar."

"And rich. With all that money, why are you living here?" Lakeisha glances around our humble home. "I mean—no offense. It's cute and all. But from what I saw on the news, your family's loaded."

"I don't want their money," I sigh. "I prefer the freedom this brings."

"Fair enough."

"Hey—is there any way to find out if my mother visited?

Are there records of those things?"

"Sure. I can check for you," she offers. "If she came by, she'd have had to sign in."

"She insists she was there but I'm pretty sure I'd have known if she was. But there's always a chance that I'm wrong. All my life, it's been a battle between my memory and hers. Now that there's a way to confirm something, I feel like I should."

Lakeisha rises to correct my form. "Girl, that's nuts."

"Am I acting crazy? Maybe it's too paranoid… You're right."

"Not you," she assures me. "It ain't right that your mother has it so you can't trust yourself. Same as your sister."

"Well, we don't know if she's wrong yet."

"And what'll happen when you find out she lied?"

"I guess I'll need to reconsider a few things. Like: why does she always challenge my memories? And, what other times did this happen?"

"It's messed up. Your mother's one of the few people you're supposed to be able to trust in this crazy world."

IN BETWEEN

Dottie and I sit in silence for an unusually long time. My eyes trace the orange swirls on the sheer white curtains that dance lightly in the wind.

"As much as I hate to admit it, I might have missed this place a little."

She smiles. "What'd you miss about it?"

"It's just familiar and unfamiliar enough. Could be that I missed everything. That's what happens after spending three weeks without vision."

"How'd things go this past week?"

I roll my eyes and sigh. "When I got out of my catatonic state, I told Jae-Mee that in order to find the truth, I'd have to give everyone a fresh start. You know—create a baseline."

"And how has that been?"

"It may have been a little lofty."

"Did something happen?"

"Nothing out of the norm. It's just… When I planned this in my head, I expected everyone to know they could start fresh, too. Or maybe I hoped that they would. But of course they didn't. They treat me the same as they always have."

"What would happen if you told them?"

"That I've wiped the slate clean?" Dottie nods and I snicker. "Hilarious. I'm still building up my strength. I'm not ready for World War III."

"Why would that start a war?"

"Announcing a clean slate will make them angry that I thought one was needed. Then I'd have to say more."

"Don't you think they'd want to know?" Dottie looks at me quizzically.

"Of course not. That's one of the problems. I'm not allowed to have issues with anything they do. It makes them angry."

"I have to say, I'm impressed by this awareness."

"I've had a lot of time to think."

"Tell me what else you understand about the way your family functions."

"They can never be wrong. And they have a deep fear of judgment—which is ironic, because they're hyper-judgmental of everyone else."

"People tend to be concerned that others do what they do or want to do—like when an unfaithful person's paranoid that their partner's cheating. We call it projection."

"Why is that? They just can't see themselves?"

Dottie nods. "It's quite common, unfortunately."

"Kind of like me and my abandonment issues."

Dottie narrows her eyes. "I don't get the connection."

"I was always so afraid I'd be left that I'd end up doing things to make people leave. A self-fulfilling prophecy, maybe."

"You didn't make people leave you. Your mother made that choice on her own."

"To get me to comply." My eyes find the white porcelain cat. I stare at it while chewing the inside of my cheek. "When I didn't, I backed her into a corner and she didn't know what to do."

"So, it was your fault?"

"In a way."

"Shay, a daughter is allowed to ask questions without being frozen out of the family. Didn't this happen several times?"

"But I challenged her. We all have our limits."

Dottie crosses her legs and pushes up her glasses. "I thought we were making progress, but don't you see? You're back to your old way of thinking."

I consider her words. "Am I crazy? I'm sorry. I can't keep my head straight."

"You're not crazy. You were conditioned over time not to challenge your parents because of what might happen. And then it did. It's not your fault that your mother hurt you."

"She didn't do it on purpose though. Right? No mother could want to hurt her daughter that way. My mother's not perfect but she's not evil."

"Well," sighs Dottie, sitting upright, "there's a lot in between the two poles."

GRATITUDE

It feels like I'm being reborn into a world that's crumbling down all around me.

Each morning I wake to a quick flash of panic before realizing I'm not in the hospital anymore. I can open my eyes, yawn loudly, stretch my limbs, tell the man of my dreams that I love him, and pat my adorable cat. I can eat whatever I want. My range of motion is improving. I haven't felt so full of hope since I was a young child. But at the same time, everything that I've ever wanted to believe about my family is caving in.

I just want it to be better. Why can't things be better?

Jae-Mee opens his eyes and catches me staring off into space. He asks, "What's wrong?"

"Nothing," I lie. "Everything's perfect."

He stretches his arms above his head and cracks his neck. "You're full of shit."

"Okay… Maybe not everything."

"Nothing has to be perfect, you know." He stretches and twists towards me. "It's okay for things to be flawed."

"I know. I just want you to realize how grateful I am to be here, awake and alive, and with you."

"I know you are," he says, giving my leg a squeeze. "It doesn't need to be proven. Nothing's going to cancel that out.

It seems like you're always afraid to say what's not good, as if it'll take away from what is."

Paisley climbs up onto my stomach and rests her belly on mine. Her eight-pound body buzzes on me, easing the anxiety stirring within.

Jae-Mee rests his face on my shoulder. "I promised myself if you made it back home, I'd try harder to connect. So, talk to me."

Tears drip down my cheeks. I discreetly wipe them away, pretending I'm pushing the hair from my eyes. "I think my family's been lying to me."

"About what?"

"Maybe everything. I don't know."

"What makes you think that?" Jae-Mee asks, moving his head back to his own pillow to get a good look at my face.

"Mother says she visited me in the hospital. And Myra claims she was there three times a week. I know it sounds petty but they're telling me I don't remember and it pisses me off. It's what they've always done to confuse and dismiss me."

"What else?"

"Too much. I thought about it all when I was in the hospital. It's not like I could do much else. A lot of memories surfaced—things I'd been trying hard not to think about, because I just wanted to be grateful for what I had. I haven't made sense of it all. But I know... some things just aren't right."

"What do you remember?"

"I'm still not sure. But when I'm ready, I'll tell you. I swear."

Jae-Mee places his head back down on my shoulder and begins to pat Paisley, too. Sometimes our hands overlap. He says, "I love you."

I chuckle. "Me with all of my problems?"

"Yes—you with all of your problems."

I rest my hand on top of his, which is on top of the cat. "Guess I'm pretty lucky after all."

BIRTHRIGHTS

Lakeisha guides my walker as I push through a round of supported moves with my back against the wall. It feels great to be getting stronger. I welcome the sensations of soreness and fatigue, the feeling of a really deep stretch, and even the burn of an overworked muscle.

"I think you're nearly ready to ditch the chair," she announces.

"I was hoping you'd say that. Do you think I'll be able to do yoga soon?"

"Sure. We can try a few things. Just don't go doing anything without a spotter. Transitions can be tricky since your stabilizing muscles are still weak."

She watches me alternate lunges with the walker across the room.

"Hey—did you get a chance to look into those records?"

"As a matter of fact, I did," she says, crossing her arms.

"Okay," I sigh. "What'd you find?"

"Finish this round and take a seat."

I do what she says.

"So, Myra visited twice before you woke. And Jack came once with a friend." She lifts her eyes to catch mine. "But there's no record of your mother visiting at all."

"Is there any chance that could be wrong?"

"Well, there's always a chance. But these records are probably legit."

I take a deep breath and exhale through my nostrils. "I was afraid you'd say that."

"You'd rather have remembered it wrong?"

"You sound like my shrink. But yeah. Kind of."

Lakeisha inches over and holds my forearm. "Listen, I have two girls of my own. If either of them were hurt, you bet your left titty I'd be right there with them. Nothing could keep me away."

I force a smile. "Well, they're lucky girls."

"No they ain't. Having a good mother isn't lucky. It's a birthright."

I can't speak out of fear that I'll cry. I don't want to pity myself now, and especially not in front of Lakeisha. I take a deep breath and exhale through puffed cheeks. "I appreciate your help."

"We'll get you in better shape than ever. You're still young. You've got so many great things in store. To hell with them."

"Yeah," I say, without much conviction.

"Look, you can either let the wind keep blowing your hair into your face, or you can turn to face the wind head on."

Rolling my eyes, I ask, "What's that supposed to mean?"

"That's up to you."

"Jesus," I moan. "I don't know if you sound more like my shrink or a meme."

WHO WE CHOOSE

I need to get out. The apartment's beginning to feel like the hospital room. I wheel myself outside, down the ramp, and work my way down the street.

My spine straightens, reaching up towards the sun. The cool air sweeps through my body, waking all of my senses. And the rhythm of pushing myself over concrete reminds me of my own strength.

Here I am, out in the world all alone, getting by. I take in the scene. The lavender flowers in the neighbor's garden are hanging on. Someone on the street bought a bright yellow sportscar. The leaves are starting to turn reddish-orange. A sad, half-filled scarecrow sits on a white plastic chair on a porch.

Rolling around the block, I consider my lack of friends. My social media accounts would make you think I'm surrounded by besties, but I've been too overwhelmed to get back on there. I dread the well-meaning, diminishing remarks that I've learned to expect. In the meantime, no one's been calling.

I have a habit of taking on friends when they need me and losing them when they don't. They tend to reach out when they're in a struggle. I'll spend countless hours online or on the phone, providing reassurance. However, the few times I've shown my own weakness were met with shrugs and platitudes.

One of my more recent friends got drunk and yelled at me in a bar last year. It had something to do with how my posts online—that had nothing to do with her—made her feel she was being judged. She unleashed a lot of pent-up anger that I didn't understand but could tell were drops from a deeper well. I sent her a few messages hoping to smooth things over, but just like Mother, she never responded.

Why do I choose these people? Why do they choose me?

Looking back on my graveyard of friendships, I stumble upon Shae. There's a deep pang in my chest. Working my way back up the ramp to the apartment, I decide to seek her out.

I call her old number and get someone else's voicemail. I Google Shae Cooper in Vermont but nothing comes up. Remembering her father's name, I find a list of results and try the first one.

"Michael Cooper," says the voice on the other end of the line.

"Hi. Do you have a daughter named Shae?"

"No…"

"Okay, thanks."

I hang up and try the next.

"Hello?" says a familiar voice.

"Is this Mike Cooper?" I begin.

"Yes, it is. Who's calling?"

"Hi, Mr. Cooper. This is the other Korean Shay. Do you remember me?"

He pauses a moment to think. "Ah, Shay! Of course I do. How've you been?"

"Well, that's a really long story."

"It's nice to hear from you. I imagine you're looking for Shae?"

"Yeah. I'm trying to track her down. It's been ages."

"I'm sure she'd love that," he tells me. "Do you have a piece of paper?"

I write down her number and circle it three times.

"How's life?" he asks. "Are you married? Any kids?"

"Um, no and no," I report. "Life's been… interesting. I'll spare you the details."

"Are you okay?"

"I will be. How are you and Mrs. Cooper?"

"Better than ever. We're divorced now, though. Funny how it works that way sometimes."

"Oh! Well, that's nice." I struggle for words.

"I'll let you go and call Shae," he says, chuckling. "It's good to talk to you, Shay."

"You too, Mr. Cooper."

I hang up and dial Shae's number.

"Hi! You've reached Shae Livingston. I can't take your call right now, but please leave your number and I'll be in touch."

I clear my throat before the beep. "Shae? This is your old friend Shay. I tracked you down through your dad. My number should come up on your phone so call me back when you can. I'm really looking forward to being back in touch. I've missed you."

When I hang up, I wheel myself into the bedroom where I find Paisley rolling around on the bed. I maneuver myself next to her, stretching out. She climbs onto my chest and sits upright, peering down at me.

I tell her, "Momma's gonna make some changes 'round here."

FACING THE TRUTH

Dottie and I sit diagonally across from one another in silence. The hollowed-out air used to make me anxious, and I rushed to fill it with whatever sprung to mind. Now I wait till I know what I want to discuss before starting.

"Did I ever tell you about the time Mother convinced me I was crazy?"

I watch her expression shift slightly before steadying itself.

"I think I was about sixteen," I continue. "I can't recall what I was asking, but I'm pretty sure it had to do with the past. Anyway, I remember her reaction vividly. She snapped. She went off on me, but I tuned out her words and shrunk a few layers deep into my shell. And then her face went eerily blank as she told me I was schizophrenic."

"Schizophrenic?" Dottie echoes.

"She said that my memories were hallucinations and that I can't trust my own mind. She ran downstairs to grab an encyclopedia and shouted each symptom she thought I had—moodiness, paranoia, spending too much time alone. But mostly, remembering things that never happened."

"Did she take you to a doctor?"

"Nope. She said we couldn't trust them—that they'd lock me away. She told me she'd treat me instead."

"What was her treatment?" Dottie asks, eyes widening

slightly.

"She was more strict, I guess. I had to keep my bedroom door open at all times. She'd find and read my diaries, going over each thing that she swore I concocted in my twisted-up head. She was always looking for some kind of proof."

"And you believed her?"

"I think I did. Or, maybe I just wanted to because it was simpler."

"Simpler than what?"

"The idea that she didn't want me to trust my own mind? Or that she was the one who couldn't be trusted? I don't know."

"Did you ever seek treatment before coming to me?"

"No. I bought into Mother's fears. She'd say all they ever do is blame it on the parents. They're all quacks."

Dottie raises the corners of her mouth.

"I made a fool of myself. I told all my old friends, thinking it excused some of my strange behavior. And later, when boyfriends said I was crazy, I believed them. I was always so quick to believe I was the one who was wrong. You know— this is probably why I've been afraid to get too close to people."

"You must've really wanted to trust your mother," she stresses, switching the cross of her legs.

I look up, quizzically. "Do you think I could be? Schizophrenic? Is it possible that I might be crazy, and everything I think I remember is a lie?"

"I'm one hundred and ten percent sure you're not schizophrenic. Maybe even one hundred and twenty."

"What if I'm just that good?"

"No."

"So, what's wrong with me? You must have a diagnosis by

now. I see you jotting things down." I want to provoke her.

Dottie shrugs. "You're depressed. Honestly, I think you're a fairly healthy person responding to the environment you were in. You're coping with clashing ideas of what you've been told versus what you're uncovering to be true—things you may have known all along on some level."

"Can't you just open my brain and put things in order for me?"

She smiles. "You're doing that on your own. It's hard work, but you're doing it and I'm proud of you."

I cringe.

"Does that make you uncomfortable—when I tell you I'm proud of you?" I nod yes, still cringing. "What does that evoke in you?"

"Eh," I grunt. "It's like... well... I don't want to believe it. On the one hand, I know it's rude for me to call you a liar. And on the other, if I believe it, does that make me full of myself? And then I'm uncomfortable, wondering what's in it for you."

"What's in it for me is your healing," she says. "Once you start trusting yourself, you'll realize your own worth."

"Realize my own worth. What does that even mean? That concept is frightening."

"Frightening how?"

"Aren't we all worth the same? Plus, my family has really high self-esteem but it doesn't make them treat people well."

"They may have an inflated sense of self-worth. Or perhaps it's a cover-up for what they lack."

I shrug.

"Once you know your own worth, you can begin to trust yourself and trust others. You're doing great. You're getting there."

"I don't know," I mumble. "The world is full of untrustworthy people. Maybe trusting is overrated."

"And that's you trying your darndest to negate a compliment and side-step your way out of the dance."

"Sorry," I laugh. "You're totally right."

"This isn't going to be easy. That's why most people don't do it."

"What are we talking about here—dancing?"

"Facing the truth," Dottie says, unflinchingly. "The real truth that lives deep inside us."

Inside, I'm scowling at how New Agey she sounds. "I suppose it's easier to go on believing what you want to believe."

"Is it?" Dottie asks, slightly rotating her head. "You tell me."

NOT FOR EVERYONE

I've been home for weeks and I've already lost some of what I've remembered. How am I supposed to trust myself and my memories if they keep disappearing?

In some respects, Mother was right about my mind.

In some respects, I miss trusting Mother, even if it meant I was batshit crazy. I decide to give her a call.

"Hello?" She answers the phone like a woman with windblown hair who just happened to pass by it as it rang.

"Hi Mother."

"Shay!" The excitement in her voice sends the butterflies in my stomach into a frenzy. "I was just thinking about you! Great minds think alike. I was chatting with Mrs. Anderson at the grocery store and her daughter's a bigwig in pharmaceuticals. They make a ton of money. I told her you're a designer and to have Laura get in touch if they ever need help. I bet you could use some making up for lost time."

"Actually, I'm doing all right. Art's been good to me."

"But that's small potatoes compared to what Laura could land you. You've got to keep setting your sights higher. Just keep an open mind. Okay? You never know."

I realize this is the first private conversation we've had in ages.

"Alright. I will."

Mother launches into her updates, as if I'd been gone for years. "Myra's keeping busy trying to make Graham famous. God love her. Jack's head over heels in love. He's finally grown up and become a man. Lord knows it took him long enough. I'm not sure about her yet. Did you see her at the party? You know, I think I might have babied him—treated him too well—to be honest. And, you've heard Tamara's having another boy? I'll tell you—she's going to have her hands full. Of course I'll help, I always do. That girl's not too bright, poor thing. She can't help it. She was saved by her looks. She came from such poverty. I don't think her father has any of his own teeth. Hopefully she inherited her mother's."

I'm unsure of what to add to the conversation.

"It's going to be a pretty full house here," she continues. "But don't let that stop you from coming back. You know there's always room for you—and Jae-Mee, if you're still together. We'd love to have you."

"Of course we're still together," I tell her. "I think we might always be."

It's her turn for uncertainty. "Well, he's a nice enough guy, good-looking… I never in a million years would've imagined you ending up with another Oriental. But as long as you're happy."

"I am," I assure her, wishing I had the courage to say we prefer to be called Asian. "I've never been so happy with anyone." I don't tell her she never imagined me with another Asian because we never lived where there were any.

"Well, you sure chose some losers," Mother laughs. "Myra, though—she's always been lucky with men."

"She's divorced twice."

"Yeah, but they were good men. They all came from good

stock. I saw Bobby the other day at the post office. He's got two beautiful children, a nice wife, and big house. I wouldn't dare tell your sister, though."

"Why? She's happy with Graham… Isn't she?"

"As happy as she can be. He's a beautiful man but I don't know if he really has that much talent. It's a cutthroat business. Only the best survive. Myra should've gotten into modeling much sooner. I'm sure she would've been a household name by now. I was afraid it would encourage her eating disorder."

"Do you ever regret giving up your modeling career?"

"I don't believe in regrets," Mother blurts. "Besides, if I did, I'd never have had any of you kids. Maybe we would've still adopted, but it might not have been you. And it definitely wouldn't have been the same."

"True," I consider.

"I gave my life for you kids and I'd do it again in a heartbeat." I can hear the smile through her voice. "Once I had Ivan, I knew I had to keep going. Being pregnant was like being the mayor. Everybody loves a pregnant woman. They can't wait to open doors, help you out with your bags… When you're pregnant, you're a Goddess. You're carrying life."

My heart softens as I listen to Mother go on about children. Disarmed, I say, "I might want to have one or two someday."

"You? Oh… I never thought you'd want one. And you're kind of getting up there in age for your first."

"Why wouldn't I want one?"

"You always seemed to have other things on your mind."

"I could never imagine having kids with my exes. But Jae-Mee's different. And a lot of adoptees find having their own kids healing. Seeing someone look like you for the first time… I can't really imagine."

"Well, be careful," Mother warns. "It's not something to enter lightly. You really do have to put your whole life on hold—which you've already just done. It's a lot of work. Kids change everything. You want to make sure you're up to the lifelong challenge. And you really must consider your mental shortcomings."

I gloss over her continued insinuations of my insanity. "But you just said how wonderful it is to have kids—to be pregnant, carrying life and all that."

"Oh, it is," Mother says, with that magical warmth returning to her tone. "But it's not for everyone."

When we disconnect, I wonder if the idea of me having my own family threatens Mother somehow. Or, if she really believes I'd be terrible at it.

TWO MILLION DOLLARS

Lakeisha storms in, the door flying open and slamming behind her. I hear her stomp through the foyer to where I'm sitting, blowing smoke through her ears.

Placing hands on her hips, she demands, "Why didn't you tell me you were suing the hospital? Gross negligence? I had to find out from my boss! I've been coming here as a special favor—and you've said nothing about it. You blindsided me."

"I'm sorry. I really didn't think they'd do it."

"What do you mean 'they'? It's in your name!"

"My family must've done it on my behalf."

She throws her hands in the air. "We're done. They told me I can't continue our sessions."

"Why?"

"Because it looks shady as fuck! The hospital is giving your rich-ass family two million dollars. They might think I'm in on it with you for a cut. Either way, it don't look good for the hospital. And the hospital says it don't look good for me."

Lakeisha plops down on the couch.

I nearly choke out my words. "They're giving my family two million dollars?"

"That's right," she says, shaking her head.

"I'm sorry," I repeat. "Lakeisha, I had no idea. Myra told me they were considering a lawsuit, but I figured they'd come to their senses. I told her I didn't want any part of it and she said they'd do it without me. I didn't really think—"

Lakeisha cackles. "Oh, isn't that perfect! I should've known it was that evil one's plan. Well, the hospital wants to keep it out of court so they're just handing the money over."

"But you did nothing wrong. Don't settle. Take them to court and let them lose."

She looks weary as she steadies her eyes on me. "Look… in the incident with the shooter, we lost you. The circumstances were crazy but that's the truth. Andy was hospitalized elsewhere thinking of whether he wanted to file his own lawsuit, and others were home, traumatized. We were short staffed and hired a few temps. It was a hot mess. No one even noticed you were gone. And not everybody survived."

"I even told Myra that if things didn't happen as they did, my body might still be asleep in that hospital room." I want her to know I'm on her side.

"What a waste," she groans. "Why does your family need more money?"

"They never seem to think they have enough."

Lakeisha huffs, "The worst part about the whole thing is: they probably wouldn't stand a chance in court."

"Then why doesn't the hospital fight them? I don't get it…"

"With a high-profile, connected family like yours? They chose the path of least resistance." Lakeisha shakes her head some more. "They want to keep it on the DL so no one else— who might be more deserving—gets the idea. That's why it's all happening so fast."

I glance down at my knees, unsure of what to add. I want to cry.

"Well, I'm going to lose my job if I stay here much

longer," Lakeisha says, rising.

"I don't know what to say. I'm sorry it happened. It was out of my hands."

She rests her hand on my shoulder, peering down on me with sharp eyes. "Girl… I think I'm beginning to understand how you ended up in there for so long. Your family is scary. I'm surprised you've made it this far in life."

A wave of shock washes over me.

The door slams and Lakeisha is gone.

GOOD GRIEF

How to Reconcile the Loss of Someone You Really Liked:
- Roll your sorry ass into the bedroom and lie face down on the bed.
- Make sure the cat's not in the room.
- Scream into your pillow as loud as you can.
- Roll onto your back and stare at the ceiling.
- Glare at the patterns the dots of ceiling plaster create until your eyes cross and you begin to see the faces of the ones who caused the loss.
- Release a fury-filled "Gah!" banging your fists by your side a few times.
- Roll to your side, shove a pillow between your knees and squeeze it tightly against your chest.
- Consider how many others those faces in the ceiling made you lose, directly or indirectly.
- Cry pathetically—but not too intensely.
- Wipe your face. Blow your nose. Become flooded with guilt.
- Feel completely inept at everything.
- Reconsider all the choices you've ever made.
- Imagine that everyone would be better off without you.
- Unconsciously pinch the roll of fat in your curled-up stomach.

- Wonder what it'd be like to completely redo yourself with plastic surgery.
- Imagine running off to create a new life with a new identity.
- Remind yourself that it was already done for you when you were an infant.
- Ask yourself how that turned out.
- Feel guilty for not feeling as grateful as you'd like to feel.
- Wish you were adopted to another family.
- Punch your head with your fist for daring to think that.
- Remember you have a frozen pizza in the kitchen.
- Preheat the oven.
- Shove the wheelchair across the room and tip it on its side.
- Track down your black cat.
- Hug the cat to your chest as you inhale the back of her neck.
- Put on some tunes.
- Stick the pizza in the oven.
- Consider making yourself a drink.
- Stop yourself because you realize you already have too many problems.
- Sing along to sad songs off-key.
- Take the pizza out of the oven.
- Burn the roof of your mouth on said pizza.
- Eat the whole fucking pizza anyway.
- Stare at yourself in the floor-length mirror.
- Lean in to inspect all your flaws.
- Go back to bed.
- Pull the covers over your head.
- Realize you have to urinate.
- Shake your fist in the air at the Pee Gods.

- Wait as long as possible to get up.
- Crawl back into bed for as long as you can.

IF YOU COULD

I hear Jae-Mee come through the front door, throwing down his keys and sunglasses and dropping his messenger bag on the table with a thud. When his feet step towards the bed, I can't see him but feel his presence.

He calls my name. And just as I'm about to answer, he tears off the covers and says, "Holy shit. You scared the crap out of me."

"Sorry," I offer, tugging them back over my shoulders.

Jae-Mee takes off his shoes and crawls into bed. "Rough day?" he asks, with an exaggerated pout.

"Let's see," I start. "I lost my friend-slash-physical therapist because as it turns out, the hospital is awarding my family two million dollars to settle a bullshit case they've brought against them—in my name—for misplacing me for one day."

"Two million dollars? Do you think they'll give you any of it?"

"I don't want it. This might cause Lakeisha to lose her job. She has kids."

"How is it in your name?"

"They forged it. It's not the first time."

"What a shit show," Jae-Mee says, running fingers through his hair.

"And this isn't the first person my family's driven from me—directly or indirectly."

"What's their problem?"

"They're so controlling. And they think they're more deserving than the rest. They'd take all that money away from people who legitimately need it…"

"What'll you say to them?"

"I don't know," I moan. "You know how they are. I'm afraid to say anything."

Jae-Mee leans back, tucking his arms behind his head.

"What are you thinking?" I ask.

"I'm just wondering… if you could live anywhere in this country, where would it be?"

"I could never leave this area. My family would never talk to me again. They're mad enough that I'm not still at home."

"Pretend that's not an issue. Just think. Where would you live if you could?"

"Well… it's got to be on a coast. Somewhere diverse with good culture."

"So far, so good."

"I've always liked San Francisco," I say, rolling onto my back to dream with him. "I've always thought it was a place I could live."

He carries on for me. "It has everything. Good food. Lots of Asians. A decent art scene. Hills and mountains, sea lions…"

"Sea lions!" I coo, smiling wide.

"And it's just about the best in the country for tech. We could probably both get work out there."

I roll to face him and whisper, "Let's go. Let's do it, Jae-Mee. Let's move as far across the country as possible."

"That'd be Hawaii or Alaska. Alaska, I think."

"I want California." I grin.

Jae-Mee tugs me towards him. He puts on a western accent and says, "Let's get the fuck out of Dodge, baby."

With my face pressed into his shoulder, I let out a muffled, "Really? Do you think we can do it?"

"Why not? What's stopping us?"

"Let's keep it a secret. Okay? Let's just plan it and go."

Jae-Mee pulls back to search my face. "Do you think you could be happy there… with just me and no one else? Well, I guess Paisley can come, too."

I press my face back into his shoulder so he can't see my tears when I tell him, "You're all I have anyway."

THE HOLE IN THE BOAT

Since I've been home, Jae-Mee and I haven't had sex. He hasn't moved towards it and neither have I. I've been secretly relieved and a little concerned that he doesn't find me attractive anymore.

I admit this to Dottie at our next session and she asks, "Why do you think that is?"

"Maybe he got used to living with a sexless freak. Maybe he's tired of being rejected."

"And what if he did approach sex with you?"

I find my old friend, the white porcelain cat, and confess, "I guess I'm not ready yet anyway."

"What's there to be ready for?"

"Everything? I'm afraid of freaking out when he touches me and going through that whole thing again. Things have been really nice. I don't want to ruin it."

Dottie peers down her glasses. "Do you believe he loves you?"

"Yes. But you know—he also loves the cat. He doesn't want to sleep with the cat but he doesn't want to lose her, either."

Dottie tilts her head back and laughs with abandon. "I'm sorry, that was inappropriate of me," she says when she recovers. "But do you really think his love for you—his human girlfriend—is on par with his love for the cat?"

I smirk. "I guess not. I'm just saying that love comes in many forms. Maybe he's happy never having sex with me again."

"Why don't you ask him?"

"Without being ready for it if I'm wrong? I don't think so."

Dottie's tone is serious again. "You do need to get to the root of it. As you say, this began well before you fell into catatonia."

"Do I really need to? Can't whatever it is just be dealt with on another level, without the hassle of raking through my brain, digging up meaningless dirt? How about that whole flooding the mind with positivity so there's no room left for negativity?"

"How's this," Dottie starts. "You've got a hole in your boat and you don't know where it is. The boat keeps leaking, so you keep expending energy bailing it out. Maybe you'll find a crafty way to glue some tarp over the entire bottom, but that's not going to be strong enough to hold it forever. Sooner or later, that boat's going down. Now, do you want to keep going in that circle until you drown? Or do you want to find that pesky little hole and fix it for good?"

"Can't I just get a new boat?"

"'Fraid not."

My eyes are fixed on the white porcelain cat. "I might've found the hole. But maybe not."

"You're allowed to explore it—regardless of where you're at with it."

"I wouldn't want to go there if I'm wrong."

"Let's examine it. It's safe in here."

I pull the Aztec-printed blanket down and wrap it around me to soothe the goose bumps on my skin. My muscles shake.

I squeeze the blanket tightly in front of my chest.

"I've always had these weird feelings about my father," I confide in a mumble. Dottie's silent, upright in her chair. "I've always been uncomfortable around him—the way he looked at me and other girls. It never felt right. I pushed it all out of my head, but the memories filtered in when I was catatonic."

Dottie's eyes are sad, a look I can see she's trying to repress. "How so?"

"I don't know," I admit. "That's partly why I don't want to talk about it. Mother always said that if I didn't know what I was talking about, I shouldn't say anything. And I think she's right on this. It's dangerous territory."

Dottie adjusts herself slightly in her chair. "Your mother's not here now. And I'm telling you it's okay to say whatever's on your mind."

"He just made my skin crawl," I tell her, fighting back tears. "I know—it's a terrible thing to say about my father. But the way he was with Myra... Tickling her in her bikinis..."

"Well, that's certainly inappropriate."

"That's all I remember. And it's probably why we both had nightmares for years. I just never felt comfortable and at ease in that house."

Dottie hands me a box of tissues that feels much too bright and cheery for the moment, with its pastel floral print. I rest it in my lap, studying it as if I'll need to draw it from memory.

"Anything else?" she whispers.

"Nothing concrete. Just weird feelings."

"We often dissociate in order to survive difficult situations. And that can make it harder to recall in detail later."

"Dissociate? Is that like when you detach from your body?"

"That's one way to put it."

"I've done that a lot. I was wondering if being hospitalized with catatonia was like one big, long dissociation."

I pull out a few tissues and bury my head in my hands. I shake quietly to myself, horrified to be crying in front of someone else.

Dottie comes over to the couch to sit beside me. "I know this is hard but you're doing great," she tells me. "You're finally opening up this old wound that never healed right."

"But I don't want to," I manage, blowing my nose. "What if I'm making a snowball out of fake snow and it falls apart in my hands?"

"Whatever this is, I think it's your ticket. The crux of what you need to explore before you're free."

"I'm not ready."

"I think you are."

She says it with such confidence that I almost believe her.

DEMOLITION

After sharing the details of my session with Jae-Mee, I rest my head on his chest. Paisley squeezes herself in between us on the bed as we both cry without making a sound.

Sometimes comfort doesn't come from what's said but what's not.

When he leaves for work, I run through my physical therapy exercises. I call in sick and spend days in bed, feeling pathetic that I don't fully know what I'm crying about.

When the phone rings, I let it go to voicemail. I can't talk to anyone. Every inch of my body feels weighed down by a ton of bricks.

I've been moving around without the walker—partly out of defiance. I was doing alright, but climbing into bed I miscalculate and crash to the floor. I must've blacked out for a second or two. My head spins. My heart revs. When I open my eyes, I notice a familiar, vexatious sound.

Tick tick tick tick tick tick tick.

I lift my head and look for the culprit.

Tick tick tick tick tick.

I drag myself out of bed and search for the sound, craning my neck forward—as if that will help.

Tick tick tick tick tick.

Where is that motherfucker?

Tick tick tick.

If I don't find it, I'm going to lose my mind.

Tick tick tick.

I'm bumping into things left and right, bending over to look inside drawers.

Tick tick tick tick tick tick.

Where the fuck is it?

Tick tick tick tick tick.

All around the apartment, I'm lifting things and throwing them down. It's got to be coming from somewhere...

Tick tick tick tick.

My body's on overdrive.

Tick tick tick.

I'm whipping open cabinets and drawers.

Tick tick tick tick tick.

I'm going to find you and I'm going to kill you.

Tick tick tick tick tick.

I'm opening the fridge and the freezer. I start flinging things around in there, too.

Tick tick tick. Tick.

Sharpening my ears, I back out of the kitchen and step into the living room.

Tick tick tick tick tick.

I crank my head forward again, honing in on the sound like a raptor stalking its prey.

Tick tick tick.

Tearing the pillows and cushions off the couch, out of the corner of my eye I catch something fly across the room.

Tick tick tick.

I twirl myself around and crash down on my knees, crawling towards it. It's a watch. I don't recognize it.

TICK. TICK. TICK.

Clutching the watch, I steady myself up on my own two feet. Every muscle in my body is working to propel me towards the hall closet.

TICK. TICK. TICK. TICK. TICK.

I pull a hammer out of the closet. I take it and the watch and walk myself outside to collapse on the concrete steps.

TICK. TICK. TICK.

Placing the watch face up on the step, I swing the hammer as hard as I can.

TICK.

I demolish the motherfucker in about forty blows.

THE BOTTLE BURSTING TO POP

"He was the monster; our nightmare," I tell Dottie. "I think on some level, I connected the dots that day I was hospitalized—or I started to. And that's why I went blank. The shock was too great."

"Tell me what happened."

"I never lie on the couch. It's not a good couch for lying down. I usually go to the bedroom—but for some reason, not that day. I must've heard it ticking from under the cushion."

"What was it?"

"Jae-Mee's watch. A birthday gift from his dad."

Dottie nods, prompting me to continue.

"I went into a frenzy. When I went back inside, I saw that I'd torn the place apart. But the thing is, I couldn't possibly have heard it from the bedroom. There must've been something in my brain coaxing me to remember—maybe because of our last session."

"What did it want you to remember?"

"The big clock in the living room ticking. I used to hear it when it was about to happen. It was always ticking, of course. But I only ever noticed it when something changed in the middle of the night—when I sensed something wasn't as it should be. Maybe a creak in the floor or some other sound. And then I'd hear that clock tick and know to play dead—

well, asleep. It gave me something to focus on. It was the clock my parents got for their wedding." I shiver.

Dottie purses her lips and exhales as if she'd been holding her breath this whole time.

I feel my face start to contort and I lose all control. I can barely squeak out my words. "I heard what he was doing to Myra. I should've saved her but I didn't. I just let it happen!"

"You were a child. It wasn't your responsibility to stop it. You probably didn't fully understand."

"But nobody else stopped it!"

"Nobody saved you either," she whispers.

I grab the tissues from Dottie's outstretched hand and tear a cluster out of the box. I cover my entire face with them, horrified by my loss of composure.

Dottie says, quietly, "It's not your fault, Shay."

"Why didn't Mother stop him? She had to know! Looking back, it all makes sense. Her irrational jealousy... It was so obvious. How could I forget for so long?"

Dottie waits for me to settle down. "You've solved the mystery. Now you know the truth—what pushed you over the edge. It was a total shock to your system."

"But, how could I not remember till now? How could my mind deceive me? For all that time?"

"Your mind was protecting you. You weren't ready to face it yet. But it was in your body language, and lurking below the surface. I believe that's why you started acting out during intimate times, and why you never enjoyed sex unless you were intoxicated. The memory was starting to rumble and make itself known."

"How am I ever going to have a healthy sex life again?" I cry. "Jesus... I'm ruined!"

"You're not ruined. It'll take some time but you'll get

there. You have to acknowledge that what happened to you back then was abuse—and not the same as what happens between you and Jae-Mee."

"Why did I become catatonic?"

"We can't know for sure. But dissociating is how you survived the initial trauma. You said your body shut down and you feigned sleep? Perhaps that became your refuge to avoid the truth?"

"I'm so stupid for not facing this shit until now. All those flowery poems and cards..."

"You're incredibly brave. Remember that fresh start you wanted? Maybe it's not as you'd hoped, but you now have that chance. You can reshape your life into anything you choose."

I lift my head, blowing my nose. "Jae-Mee and I talked about moving to California."

"California's beautiful. I went to school out in Berkeley."

"Maybe we can start over?" I ruminate. "Take the cat. Maybe get a dog, have a kid, and forget about my whole crazy family, the past..."

"That's an option. You have many. Life can be just beginning."

"Is it possible? Can I ever move on—inside, though?"

Nodding soberly, Dottie says, "People do it all the time. There'll be some heavier days and weeks than others but overall, life can be good. Perhaps better than you've ever imagined."

The movie Eternal Sunshine of the Spotless Mind pops into my head. I tell Dottie, "I wish there was a way to just forget about everything—all the shit that's happened in my life. Isn't there a pill that makes you forget? Or some way to pluck it all from my mind? I want to be dumb again. Ignorance was bliss."

"There's not a single thing you've shared," Dottie says, while adjusting her gold-rimmed glasses, "that convinces me that your life has ever been blissful."

TO BELIEVE

I spend a lot of time mulling over what to say to Myra. I compose an email that I edit around fifty times. I know serious conversations are typically appreciated in person, but there's no way I'd ever get more than a sentence in that way. So I finish the email and send it.

Hey big sis,

I've been struggling with how to approach this. No matter how it's said, I realize it'll be difficult to process. Since I've always been better at writing than speaking, here goes.

When I was in the hospital, I had nothing to do but think. Even when I didn't want to think, things came to me. I was visited by memories I'd tried to forget and other things that I couldn't see clearly before. Maybe it didn't feel safe to remember them out in normal life, so they visited like ghosts while I slept.

Since I've been out of the hospital, I've been trying to move on and just appreciate the here and now. But I guess I've gotten to that point where my mind won't let me gloss over the truth anymore. The closet I've been shoving things into to forget is overflowing. It's no longer a choice. I can't carry on living a lie.

I always wanted to believe we had a wonderful family—the

best. Mother was an angel and Father was a saint. And while on some level, those things are true, I now see that it's not the whole truth.

As much as I love her, Mother has been manipulative throughout our lives. She's always found ways to get what she wanted, to make us believe we were wrong and she was right, no matter the cost we'd pay. And Father… This is even harder to say… but Father was—at the very least—sexually inappropriate.

I understand now why you'd always say you never had nightmares. I used to think that was all they were because I'd force myself to zone out and wake up convincing myself it was all a bad dream. I didn't trust that what happened could've been real. And when I told Mother, she told me I was sick and evil for my imagination. She eventually came up with the idea that I was schizophrenic. But I think she knew what was happening. Maybe she was jealous, and that's why she took things out on us.

I know how hard this must be to read. It took me this long to be able to see it as truth. I think I've known it all along though, on some level. I almost didn't say anything but felt I owed it to you. Maybe once you see how badly you've been hurt, you'll be able to find the true happiness I seek for myself.

I know I've always been a pain in the ass to you. You never asked for a little sister. I wish I could've been more of what you wanted. Anyway, I hope you're able to receive this with deep consideration. I'm here if you want to talk.

Love you,

Shay

Five minutes after it's sent, Myra calls. I take a deep breath and answer the phone, unsure of what to expect.

Myra launches in, screaming so loudly I can hardly make out her words. I pull the phone away from my ear. "What the fuck do you think you're doing? Have you lost your mind? It was bad enough you played dead for a month, but now you try to tear the family apart with this shit? Honest to God! This is outrageous! How can you believe those disgusting things about Mother and Daddy? You're obscene! Maybe you better check yourself back into the psych ward because you're crazy!"

"But, Myra—"

"Who the fuck is putting these ideas in your head? That therapist? I'm going to sue her! She's going to be living on the streets when I'm done with her! Give me her name!"

"I don't feel comfortable with that."

"Well, I don't feel comfortable with this shit! I mean—what the fuck did I just read?"

"Myra, she didn't put any ideas in my head. These memories started the day I became catatonic."

Myra shouts, "Bullshit! It's all bullshit, Shay! Is this the thanks they get for taking you in and giving you a privileged life? You accuse them of this?"

I take a deep breath and release it slowly. My voice is calm. "Myra, I know this must hurt. You don't want to believe it. You don't want to think of them like this. I don't either."

"Then don't! You're fucking insane, Shay! And you're killing this family! Is this what you want? Is this how you repay them—and us? Mother was right about you! You're a schizo!"

I say, "Myra... Myra..." but the phone goes dead.

PREEMPTION

I've been shivering ever since that call with Myra. Not even a hot shower can make me feel warm. I run a hot bath and slip into it, but even the burn of it enveloping my skin feels like frostbite. I bury myself beneath layers of clothing and tuck my shaking body into bed.

I wonder if there's a chance Dottie could be overlooking my severe schizophrenia. I imagine Dottie as an unqualified hack with a counterfeit degree framed on her wall. Under the covers, I Google her name on my phone, hoping to find some incriminating information. It'd be so much better for everyone if Dottie and I were wrong and my family was right. I could forgive Dottie and my family could forgive me.

No matter how much I will things to be simple, they aren't.

No matter how hard I try to convince myself that I'm crazy, I know that I'm not.

I cry until there are no tears left. I go numb. I am void of emotion.

My phone buzzes. There's a text from my cousin Samantha—someone I used to confide in now and then. She's ten years older and I've always admired her.

The text reads: I'm here for you, cousin. I don't know what's going on with your family, but please talk to me when you're ready. XOX

And just as I'm wondering how Samantha could know anything is happening with my family, I receive another text. It's from Ivan: You're dead to us. Why don't you just off yourself and do us a favor?

Paisley must hear my heart thumping from across the apartment because she races in to see me. Snaking her way under the covers, she presses herself against me and purrs.

The phone rings. It's Jae-Mee. I emit a shaky hello.

"Have you been online today?"

"No…" I say, suddenly panicked.

"Take a deep breath," he advises, "and don't worry. Anyone who knows you will know it's all lies. I'll be home in a few hours. We'll handle it. Love you."

"Love you," I echo.

I go online to see hundreds of notifications. My chest fills with overwhelming dread. When I click the notifications icon, at the top of my feed is a status update from Myra that I'm tagged in.

Attn: Friends of my adopted sister Shay Stone. I'm writing to warn you that my sister has lost her mind. When she was young, our mother realized she was suffering from schizophrenia. We wanted to protect her from the stigma and social ostracization, so we tried to help her on our own. Unfortunately, she has resisted our help for decades, endangering herself and others. If you look up schizophrenia and catatonia, you'll see they go hand in hand. Although we love our sister, daughter, and friend, she can't be trusted. She's a terrible liar, often believing her own ugly imagination. I've sadly learned that she's beyond help. With any luck, she'll be institutionalized and treated by professionals. With much love,

I advise you to steer clear of her. Don't believe her words—as convincing as they may seem. She's not who you think she is. She's not even who SHE thinks she is. Any encouragement will only worsen her state. Let us pray for her from afar.

I click on the comments and read the following:
- We're praying for you, Shay!
- I'm so sorry to hear this! Praying for your family, Myra!
- This saddens me deeply.
- I always knew she was a little 'off.' Still sad, though.
- Don't give up hope!
- There are many studies on adoptees and mental illness. Sorry to hear it's touched your family, too.
- Oh no, Myra! Your family has struggled so much with her!
- Hate to say it, but this is why adoption is bogus. Genes matter.
- No good deed goes unpunished! Hugs to you, Myra. Stay strong!

There are several more comments coming in but I've seen enough. I close the app and tuck my phone under the pillow.

PLAN A

I'm revisited by suicidal fantasies—my old friends. I could always rely on them in the past. They were caped heroes, promising to take my hand and lift me out of my misery forever. Perhaps I saw them as permanent dissociation.

A lot of people say suicide is selfish, but that's just not true. The biggest reason I've contemplated it was for the sake of others. I've always been too much trouble. I drag everyone around me into my pit of despair.

Jae-Mee deserves better. He'll never leave. He's too good and too loyal. He's a beautiful, caring, and intelligent man. He should be having mind-blowing sex with a healthy, happy woman who can satisfy all his needs. Life with me will never measure up to what he could have without me.

Myra was right—I tampered with the family's normalcy from the day I arrived. I stole an ordinary family from her and Ivan, and later, Jack. They'll never be able to look back on the regular family life they would have had if it weren't for me.

Mother never asked for the complicated mess I'd bring. All she wanted was to save a child in need. But I couldn't fit into her mold. And what's worse is I made her feel insecure when her own husband looked my way.

Father would be relieved if I were gone.

If there were a clean suicide that wouldn't traumatize

anyone, I'd have done it long ago. But I always get hung up on ruining the life of the one who'd find my remains.

And then I remember assisted suicide. It's legal in some places if you qualify. It would be a great act of compassion to me and everyone in my life if I could go that route. No one would need to find me. I could leave letters for everyone and arrange for my disposal. They won't be troubled to do a thing.

Over the next two days in bed, I research my plan. I get lost in a zone of Internet searches. All I'd need is ten thousand dollars to go to Zurich and convince them I deserve their help. I could falsify documents—and maybe pay an amateur actor to play my doctor on a phone I would purchase for them. I just need a few thousand more to make it happen. If I take on one decent freelance project, I'll have it within a month if I hustle.

Jae-Mee will understand. He'll be hurt for a while, but over time he'll see that I did it out of love. I'd rather he suffer a few more months than a lifetime with me.

How much can one suffer? And how much more suffering of my own do I owe?

"We don't owe anyone our suffering," Jae-Mee said. And now I believe it.

It's not fair for society to guilt people into living in pain, just because it makes them more comfortable.

I have to believe that if anyone really knew the pain inside me, they'd forgive me for doing what I have to do. And they'll see that I did it in the most compassionate way. If they don't, it won't matter to me when I'm gone.

Jae-Mee is delicate with me, giving me space. Seeing the fear in his eyes guts me. I just want to make life better for him. I take comfort in knowing my plan.

I don't shower and barely eat when he brings me food. I

feel like a poor, pathetic dog. He doesn't push me or make me do much—except honor my commitment to appointments with Dottie.

CERTAINTY

Dottie sits patiently with her ever-so-calm and undemanding presence. We've been marinating in several minutes of silence. The air thickens. I walk over to the bookshelf and grab the purple stress ball.

"Looks like you're recovering well, physically," she observes, ignoring my unkempt hair and greasy face.

I take a seat on the couch, pressing the ball between fingers before slamming it as hard as I can.

"I just wanted to see if it bounced." Her expression remains neutral. I ask, "Would you be willing to stake your career on your opinion that I'm not schizophrenic?"

"Why would I do such a thing?"

"Because my family is coming after you," I warn. "They were just awarded two million dollars from the hospital. They get pretty much whatever they want."

"Did they take the hospital to court?"

"They didn't even have to. All they needed was a good enough threat."

"And why would they come after me?"

"Because they can't handle that I know the truth and they think it's your fault." I fidget with the stress ball some more. "Myra slandered me on Facebook to attack my credibility. They're saying I'm certifiable. They announced it to my friends, coworkers—everyone. It's a preemptive strike before I get a chance to say anything."

"They must be afraid of your power."

"Power?" I scoff. "What power? They have all the power—as usual. They have safety in numbers. Once again, I'm the odd man out. Who's the world going to believe?"

Dottie says, "You have no idea how much power you have. Think about it. What have they been afraid of all along? They've been afraid of you knowing and speaking the truth. Your mother went out of her way to make you think you can't trust yourself."

"So, you're absolutely certain?"

I study her face as she swears, "I'm absolutely certain. You are not schizophrenic. It's possible you may remember some things slightly different from how they were. Everyone does. But your memories and behaviors add up and corroborate each other."

"I wish I were schizophrenic," I admit.

"I understand."

My phone buzzes and it's Myra again. I silence it and tell Dottie, "They're harassing me. I get texts and voice messages telling me what a terrible disappointment I am—that I'm sick, crazy, and better off dead."

"Sounds like it's time to set some boundaries."

"They won't even hear me out."

"If they won't listen, find another way to make your boundaries clear. Block their numbers or change yours. Disconnect from their social media accounts. Do whatever you need to reclaim your own space and sanity."

"You have no idea how much worse things will get if I cut them off. If I block their numbers, they'll be banging down my door. There's no escape."

Dottie pushes up her glasses. "Didn't you say you were considering relocating?"

Throwing the purple stress ball from one hand to the other, I tell her, "The timing is tricky. We'd have to move fast. The only way to escape them is to get the timing just right."

"What's stopping you?"

"Logistics. And maybe digesting the reality that this is actually happening."

"I appreciate that it's difficult."

"You appreciate?" I laugh. "Difficult? We're talking about me running away from my entire family and never speaking to them again."

"What are you really losing? And, who's to say you'll never speak again?" Dottie counters. "Perhaps there'll come a day when you can communicate in a safe, balanced way. Maybe in time, everyone can relax and have a chance to consider you more reasonably. In the meantime, you need to carve out a bit of space and sanity for yourself if they won't work with you. How you do that is up to you."

I throw the ball in the air and let it land on the couch beside me.

"Isn't there a saying about how you can't run from your problems?"

"There are many sayings," Dottie starts, switching the cross of her legs. "Most of them are shallow attempts to justify what you want to believe. They're often taken out of context— much like what you just did right there. Running away from your problems is what you used to do. Giving in would be running away. Right now, you're confronting things. And that's why your family is so afraid."

PLAN B

While I've been wallowing in my secret world of plans, Jae-Mee's been devising his own. When he picks me up from therapy he says, "Fuck it, Shay. Let's go to California. I've got some money and you do, too. We can pack up a few things, donate the rest, and be gone within the week."

"That's impossible."

"It's not impossible," he says. "Do you trust me?"

I pause for a moment and say, "Yes."

I decide his plan is worth a shot. If it doesn't work, I'll still have Zurich.

When I call to inform Art Starr that I won't be returning, I take no offense at the relief in his voice.

We pare our belongings down to two suitcases, a guitar, two laptops, Paisley's small bag of cat stuff, and two boxes to ship to storage. Jae-Mee arranges for a non-profit to come take the rest. I don't know what he worked out with the landlord, but we've got the little hatchback packed in two days.

Backing out onto the road to freedom, I see Jack standing in the middle of it. He waves. I roll down my window.

He looks worried. "What's going on, sis?"

I've always had a soft spot for Jack. Mother knows this. He's a sweet, gentle soul. But I can't fully trust him. He's too loyal to Mother and the lot of them. So, I lie. "We're going away for a couple of weeks. We rented a cabin in Vermont to get some fresh air and recharge."

Jack looks hurt. "How come you didn't tell the family?"

I sigh and Jae-Mee turns off the motor. "Haven't you seen what Myra's telling the world? She and Ivan have been sending me one hateful message after another. I need a break. There's no talking to them right now."

"Mother asked me to come by. She's worried sick."

And then I understand. I snap at him. "If Mother's so worried, she can call or visit on her own."

"She's afraid you'll be too upset."

"She's using you. Don't you see it?"

"Why do you have to assume the worst? She's just worried and doesn't know how to approach things with you."

"I think she knows a lot more than you—or any one of us have ever given her credit for. You know, she's not called once to ask how I'm doing since I've been out."

"She just talked to you last week," Jack reminds me.

"That's because I called her. And even then, all she did was rattle on about everyone else—aside from telling me I'm not fit to have kids."

"She just doesn't want to make you feel bad about being gone for so long. You know her. She just wants to move on. Why dwell on the past? You're out now. Let's be happy."

"I'm trying to be happy," I groan. "You have no idea how hard I've tried to be happy! But I can't be happy when people keep making me out to be crazy! All my life I've heard, 'you remember things wrong, you're insane.' How is anyone supposed to be happy like that?"

"You need to let it go, sis. Maybe that was what they did but it's all in the past."

"No, it's not!" I shout. "It's still very much in the present!

I'm sorry to raise my voice, but you just can't see it and I'm so tired, Jack. I'm too tired to convince you or anyone of anything. I just need to go. I'm sorry for yelling at you—and that's partly why I have to get out of here."

"I hope you have a good time," Jack offers. "And I really hope you find it in your heart to forgive and forget. We're your family, like it or not. And family is everything."

I can feel tears running down my face. "No Jack, it's not. At least it can't be for me."

"Don't be selfish, Shay. It's not like you."

I kiss my fingers and reach my hand out the window towards him. Jack turns his back and walks towards his car.

Jae-Mee starts the engine back up and we head off down old familiar roads that I've decidedly been down too many times. We sit in silence, stewing in our own thoughts, as we make our way towards new roads that hold promises I'm hesitant to believe.

Now and then, Jae-Mee places his hand on my knee.

Now and then, Paisley lets out a high-pitched meow.

In between wiping tears from my eyes, I smile.

THEY'LL FIND A WAY

I was floating in a lake with hundreds of dead bodies. There was red everywhere. I bathed in their blood. It was disgusting but I had no choice. The gunmen were scouring the lake, making sure they'd gotten everyone.

It was hard to breathe. I kept most of my mouth closed while opening the corner above water just enough to breathe through.

Nobody screamed—not even when being shot, which made it all the more eerie.

Men were pulling in bodies with large nets. My heart was racing, fearful of being dragged in with them. If they found me alive, they'd torture me—I was certain. If they found me, there'd be no escape.

From across the gray water, I heard someone gasp for air. And in seconds, machine gun rounds sounded off, echoing loudly, spilling more red.

Eventually someone shouted, "I think we've got 'em all, boss!"

I heard the men march off but kept still. There was no way to be certain they didn't leave someone behind to keep watch.

Day turned into night and into day and night again. I kept as still as I could with bodies rotting all around me. When brave enough to open the eye above water, I was thankful not to recognize anyone I knew.

I endured weeks floating among the dead before I felt safe enough to slowly float towards the shore. I don't know how I survived as long as I did out there.

Land felt strange when I touched it again. I crawled on my stomach, making my way into the brush.

Once safe, I realized I'd lost Jae-Mee and Paisley along the way. My heart pounded, hoping they were safe and not lost in that wretched water.

I did squats and leg lifts behind trees and bushes until my strength was renewed. And then in the dead of night, I ran. I didn't know where I was headed but I ran and I ran, thinking the legs underneath me would take off, leaving the rest of me crashing to the ground.

I ran out of the woods onto a paved road. I kept going, pumping legs and arms. My lungs pulsed up between my ears. Breath was cold; body, hot. I was a chemical reaction waiting to implode.

And then I saw headlights.

There was no way to be sure whether they'd lead to rescue or death so I crouched down in the gutter, hoping they'd drive on by. I thought perhaps they didn't see me. But they pulled over.

It was Jae-Mee with Paisley on the seat beside him. He said, "Found you! Get in!" I climbed into the truck and fell asleep.

When I woke in an unfamiliar room, there was a circle of faces peering down at me. Jae-Mee's face pushed its way into the middle. He said, "Sorry to do this to you, babe," and they all inched down closer.

I sit up and scream at the top of my lungs. Paisley jumps

off the bed.

Jae-Mee bolts upright beside me. "You okay?"

Heart thumping, I take in the dark all around me. Slowly, I begin to recognize the outline of the room we got for the night.

"Sorry," I whisper, with my heart in my throat. "It was just another nightmare."

He massages my shoulders.

"They're going to come after us," I tell him. "They'll never let us go."

"You're still dreaming," he whispers.

"No. My family. They'll find a way to ruin everything—no matter where we go."

He doesn't tell me they won't. He doesn't promise that he'll keep me safe. He just curls up beside me and holds me till we fall back to sleep.

One thing I've always loved about Jae-Mee is that he's careful not to state things he can't possibly know, or make promises that he can't keep.

FAMILIAR COVER-UPS

There are two unread texts from Myra. I delete them without looking. From the road, I change my phone number and block my family from all my social media accounts.

In my haste, I post:

Friends, I'm doing okay. Things have gotten out of hand with my family but I'm in good health and getting stronger each day. Jae-Mee and I are doing well and moving on the best we can. More to come, but just a quick thanks for all the thoughtful messages while I was out.

Dottie agrees to Skype our future appointments. My family hasn't tracked her down yet. She tells me she's not afraid of them. I tell her she should be.

I get a message on my Facebook account from my cousin Samantha: Call me when you can. We need to chat.

Not knowing who to trust, I restrict my number before dialing.

"Hi."

"Hey, cousin! You okay? What's going on?"

"Ugh," I groan. "It's a mess."

"So I see. I just want you to know that I'm on your side. Don't forget—I'm one of the few people who knows what your family is like from the inside."

I'd nearly forgotten that she lived with us for a year when I was young. I ask, "What do you mean?"

"That they're not what they seem. Man, I used to idolize your mother. She was like this goddess to me. And your father was so rich and mysterious. When I fell on hard times and they offered to take me in, I thought I'd won the lottery. It was wonderful living there for a while. I felt lucky."

"Lucky," I repeat.

"Yeah, I know," she says, aware of my issue with the word. "But I did. Your parents can be so great. When they're good to you, there's nothing like it. I never thought I'd be punished for lending them money."

"Wait. What?"

"I never told you? That's right—you wouldn't talk to me for a few years because your parents probably told you something else." Samantha sighs. "I lent them twenty thousand dollars. I was doing well then and figured I owed them the favor since they'd taken me in."

"When was this?" I ask, shocked.

"About twenty years ago. They said they needed to do some emergency work on the house. They were supposed to pay back in installments, but they didn't. I started asking about it and they got angry. They stopped answering my calls. I left messages, wrote letters… Nothing."

"This is vaguely familiar…"

"I was so hurt. I couldn't understand what was going on. And then I remembered some of their fallings out with others—like your godmother."

"My godmother… I think she stopped by to see me in the hospital."

"Yeah, well—they fucked her over, too. And many

others."

"How?"

"Mostly borrowing money to support their lifestyle. Of course, they never paid any of us back. It got so bad they declared bankruptcy and listed everyone who lent them money on it."

Chills rush up my spine as I tell her, "I had no idea."

"When I got that letter from you, I was gutted."

"Oh no... I really sent that?" I groan, pulling it out from my buried mental archives. "I'm sorry. It's all coming back now. They said you were harassing them for more money. They told us you were rich but needed more for some reason. They couldn't believe you'd become so entitled after all they'd done for you. Mother said she partly blamed herself for being so generous in the past."

"I figured it was something like that. I knew they'd used you to make me feel bad and stop asking for my own damn money. But I couldn't understand why they'd do that to me."

"I'm really sorry. I was young and stupid."

"You were never stupid. But you were young. And it's just how they are. They have a way of convincing people that you're the bad guy and they're the victims."

"I can't believe you're saying this."

"I'm sorry, but it's true."

"No—this is exactly what I've needed to hear: That someone else sees it; that I'm not crazy; that things weren't as they seemed."

"Shay, I was always a little worried about you in that house." Her voice trembles enough to make me fight back my own tears. "And I'm sorry I didn't help. I should've. I was an adult."

"Trust me," I console her, "I understand. What were you

going to do? They're too much of a force."

"Your father always used to say you were too smart for your own good. That used to bug the shit out of me."

"You heard that?"

"I heard more than they know. I just didn't understand it right away. There's a lot that I still don't."

We sit in silence a few beats.

"I just want you to know that you'll always have family here."

I tell her, "You have no idea how much that means."

THE MESS I'VE GOT IN ME

I've never felt so free as driving across the country, leaving most of my life behind. I have everything I need with me—my love, my cat, and my sanity. Only now do I realize how much baggage I'd been carrying around.

We pass things I've only seen before in pictures and movies—architecture, landscapes, and different ways of life. It all makes me want to cry but I fight back tears by clenching my stomach. When the pain returns, I bite my lip and curl forward.

"What's wrong?" Jae-Mee asks.

"Nothing," I claim, out of habit.

"That's obviously not true," he says, pulling into a gas station. "I mean—look at you. What do you need?"

"Nothing helps," I tell him. "Don't worry about it. I'll just ride it out."

"I'll be right back."

Keeled over, I work on my breathing. It doesn't help the pain so much as refocus my mind.

With my face down by my knees, I pick up my phone and against my better judgment, check Facebook. There are seventy-eight notifications. I navigate to my last status update. Some of the comments include:

- Glad to hear you're okay! Godspeed!

- I don't mean to judge but you're putting your family through an awful lot. Make peace with them before you regret it.
- Saw your brother's post. Unfriending you now.
- We don't get to choose our family. We live and we learn to be better people from sticking by them.
- Sending my love. <3
- Do whatever you need to do, Shay.
- And in the meantime, your sister's a wreck because of you. Why won't you pick up her calls? She loves you!
- I'd give my right arm for a family like yours. Silly girl.
- FAKE.
- Here if you need me.
- Your parents may not be perfect but they're the most precious gift God has ever given you!
- Faith: It does not make things easy, it makes them possible. Luke 1:37. Have faith that everything will work out in the end.
- One word: Ungrateful!!!!!!!!

I close the app. With my face still squished between my knees, I consider deleting my account.

Jae-Mee returns with water, Tylenol, Zantac, and Tums. He opens the car door and suggests, "Stretch a little. Maybe get some fresh air."

Climbing out, I tell him, "I'm sorry for holding us up."

"Seriously? You don't have to apologize for feeling like shit."

"Look… It's going to take a lifetime to untangle the mess I've got in me."

"Well, good thing we don't have any other plans at the moment."

ONE WORD

Everything is run through the recalibrator in my mind a few times now. Things I thought I knew, I reconsider. Ways I process information are re-examined. Who I am is once again, completely unknown.

As a poetic ceremony for my transition, I buy a balloon at a rest stop and release it to the sky. I watch till the red dot disappears from my view. I stand with my head back, gazing up at the vast blue nothing and wonder, "Now what?"

At a thrift store in Arizona, I gravitate towards a dress. Holding it at arm's length, I ask myself why I'm drawn to it. Do I really like it, or is it just something Mother or Myra would approve of?

When I stop myself from grabbing another slice of pizza, I question whether I'm full. I wonder, am I afraid to gain weight? Am I still hungry or sabotaging my own body out of fear of attention and its repercussions?

Try as I may, it's difficult to kick other people's voices out of my head. First, I need to know which are my own. It's daunting trying to reprogram what was reinforced for nearly four decades. There's going to be a few glitches along the way; some resistance. I try to be kind to myself.

I try to be kind to others but, sometimes when I think back on pieces of the past, I want to hate everyone. Sometimes I hate Mother. Sometimes I hate them all. And then I fight not to hate myself for allowing that hate into my heart.

Most days, despite everything, I think I love them—so much that it hurts. I ache for the pieces of them that were real; little moments of innocent truth.

I feel for Myra, Ivan, and Jack, who are still so invested in denial. I was like them not long ago—choosing the fantasy and distorting the facts—so it's hard to fault them. I empathize; we were all in the same psychological shit show even if we played different roles. We're each undoubtedly shaped by the ways we've experienced life growing up in that house.

And if I try to imagine the hurt Mother and Father must've known to become who they are, my breath stops. It's too much to bear.

And so I long for the family I never had. I yearn for the mother who birthed me and the one who buried me under her thumb. I crave for the fiction of the past to be true; all those fantasies painted in gold. I weep for the home to which I can never return—because it never really existed.

In a hotel room just over the border into Southern California, the three of us stretch out on the balcony overlooking the Colorado River.

"We made it to California," says Jae-Mee, cracking open a bottle of wine. We clink glasses and I instantly feel more relaxed in our destination state.

As the night goes on and the wine keeps flowing, I try to articulate all that's been snaking its way through my head.

And then Jae-Mee says, "Keurium."

"Keurium?" I echo.

He nods. "It's a Korean word. It means a state of longing for a person, memory, or place. It's a deep, heavy-hearted feeling. My halmoni taught me that word."

"Keurium," I mimic, letting it roll around on my tongue with the tart taste of the wine. "That sounds about right. I almost feel cheated that one word can sum up so much."

UNBROKEN BONDS

CA-1 is a sight to behold. Instead of worrying about making good time, we take the coastal route north through California. I marvel at the blues in the ocean as white-capped waves smash into rocky cliffs. Birds with craned necks soar through the sky. When veering from the coast, green and gold rolling hills line the highway. Sometimes we tuck into forrests. We speed past trees and plants with shapes and colors unlike the ones back east. And I discover that purple mountains are real, and not just a myth from "America the Beautiful."

Email notifications snap me out of my dreams for the near future, to find several messages from Myra and Ivan. I create a filter for my family's addresses so they bypass the inbox. This way I won't have to know they arrive unless I choose to look. Upon doing so, I stumble upon an email from Shae.

Hi Shay!

I was so excited to get your message. I've missed you so much throughout the years. I wanted to speak with you but I was going through a difficult time. You sounded so happy. I didn't want to be a bummer, so I waited to call when I was feeling better. But I guess you changed your number. Since you tracked me down the first time, I searched you online and found this address. Hope it's still active. If you get this, please call or write when you can.

Love,

Shae

I call her immediately. After attempting to summarize my past year, she shares the details of her marital problems. And she has three beautiful biological kids that she sees herself in. She tells me that I need to experience it for myself. We spend hours chatting away. So many years have passed; so much life has happened—yet our bond is untarnished.

I try my best to explain my family situation and Shae says, "Geez, I'm really sorry... but can't say I'm surprised."

"No?"

"Your mother's always been controlling. Duh. It's how we ended up apart. And your father scared the shit out of me."

"He did?"

"Oh yeah," she goes on. "I heard him being weird with your sister one day. And then it sounded like he was hitting her. I stayed in the shower, afraid to come out."

"As sad as that is to hear, it's reaffirming. In a world full of Stone supporters, it helps to know others saw it. So many people are quick to judge in their favor. Of course, it's only the supporters they've kept around. Their doubting of me fucks with my truth."

"Girl, don't let anybody fuck with your truth," Shae warns. "I learned that the hard way, too."

"It's difficult to build a baseline after so many years of being told I was wrong," I explain. "That there was something wrong with me."

"It takes time. But you'll get there."

In the blip of silence, I picture the two of us as old ladies watching the sun setting over the water. "I can't explain how good it feels to be back in touch with you. Promise we'll never disconnect again?"

"I swear on my sideways vagina," she says. And we laugh hysterically.

When the call ends, I stew in silence for a while with tears welling up in my eyes.

Jae-Mee asks, "You okay?"

I take a deep breath. "I got my friend back. Mother tore us apart when we really needed each other. Now here we are decades later, reconnected, and there's nothing she can do about it."

WE DIDN'T CHOOSE YOU

Jae-Mee has an in with an East Bay tech shop and is hired within days. I land some short-term freelance work. We rent a one-bedroom apartment on the beach in Alameda across from San Francisco.

On Mother's birthday, I sit on our balcony overlooking the bay. I picture her in a royal blue dress with birthday candles dancing in her pale blue eyes. The hair around her face sparkles as she puckers her lips to make a wish.

I open the filtered folder created for family and scroll through the list of senders. There's nothing from Mother.

Peering out at all the happy families in the sand, I realize I have almost everything I could hope for and more. Except family.

None of what I've learned about the Stones seems to matter as much as the hole they've left in my heart. Despite knowing my family is unhealthy, I miss being part of one.

I think of Mother moping around the house, hurt by my avoidance. I tell myself, I never gave her a chance to explain herself.

I can almost feel the warmth of her embrace as she wrapped her long arms around my toddler body. Those are the last real hugs I recall—beyond an obligatory lean and tap.

My finger hovers over the compose button before writing:

Happy birthday, Mother. Sorry for being out of touch. Just wanted to send a quick note to let you know I'm thinking of you and wishing you the best.

Love,

Shay

I decide that her birthday is not the time to get into things with her. Now that the ball is in her court, it's up to her whether or not she wants to converse.

The next morning, I check the family folder and see a new message from Mother.

Thanks for the birthday wishes. I didn't expect to hear from you. Glad you bothered to think of your family. Where are you? Jack stopped by the apartment and found out you no longer live there. Why wouldn't you tell your family you were doing something as big as moving? Myra says someone else answered at your old number. Did you change that, too? It seems you're actively avoiding us and I don't even know what we did to deserve this. Myra says she's investigating who's been "treating" your mental health, since clearly somebody's leading you down a wrong path. I'm praying for you, Shay. Come home and we'll take care of you again. You'll always be my daughter.

Xx

Mother

I cry for hours, rereading Mother's words. I envision packing up the new place and driving all the way back into her open arms. I fantasize about being her perfect daughter. I imagine her telling me the story about how she loved me before she knew me. And then I remember that she stopped loving me once she did. Instead, I was something she owned.

She's asking for answers—some of which I don't feel comfortable addressing. When I cool down, I spend hours crafting my reply:

Dear Mother,

I want you to know I'm doing well. I'm not ill. In fact, I'm better than ever. You don't need to worry about anyone leading me anywhere because nobody has. Everything I've been thinking and deciding has come from a sane, balanced place.

You asked why I'd leave without telling you. It's because I needed to clear my head and make my own decisions without interference. All the doubts of my memories and accusations of mental illness have done a number on me. Myra announced to my entire network that I'm schizophrenic and not to be trusted. But the thing is, I know enough now not to believe I'm the problem. I'm learning to trust myself.

I know in my heart that you never meant to hurt me. I understand that raising a family of four is a challenge, and that dealing with a transracial adoptee's complex needs must've been difficult. I know you've always done your best.

There are things I'm still trying to understand about my childhood and why you were adamant I was crazy. Maybe the truth was too hard for you too, and thinking I was crazy was more manageable. But I'm not and I wasn't. I just want you to see me as a capable individual, rather than dismiss me with the same old labels. Maybe then we can make things better.

I still love you.

Shay

I don't hear anything back for a week. I know better, but am anxious for a response. I'd almost prefer she respond with hate than not respond at all. It tugs at the insecurities I've known all the other times she kept herself from me. I forward what I'd sent, with:

Hi again. Just making sure you received the message below.

Two weeks later, I receive the following:

Well, you've kept me up every single night wondering how to respond. First off, I didn't just try my best. I did THE best. Raising you kids has been my life's work and I will not be told that I failed any one of you. Everyone's always telling me what a great mom I was and continue to be. Why can't you see it? You're too busy listening to the advice of quacks than the one group of people who actually know and care about you. No one else can judge a family they were not a part of.

I knew exactly what I was getting into when we adopted you. I was not surprised or overwhelmed by any complex issues. You never had any. There are adoptees all over the world doing well in life. And if you think you were dealt a bad hand by being sent to our family, that's not our fault either. We asked for a baby to love and you were chosen for us. We didn't choose you, so don't blame us for your problems. Why not write the adoption agency and blame them? No family is perfect. There are biological children being born into abusive homes who end up thriving. Spending your entire life wishing you could have had it better is no way to live.

Maybe you need to come home and watch the endless footage of you kids being happy and cared for. You were never a sad child. You were always happy and smiling. We went broke every year making sure you all got exactly what you wanted for Christmas and birthdays. We broke our backs trying to give you all the things we never had.

We've had a lot of hardships in our life—many you don't even know of because we didn't want to bog down our children. We've had financial struggles, "friends" and "family" who betrayed us, but no matter what, we were thankful each day for what we had and the children we were fortunate to raise. We never once regretted a thing.

You say that I never meant to hurt you and I struggle to grasp memory of any time I may have hurt you. You were the treasured child—even more than your siblings. Your father secretly favored you. You were given everything you ever wanted. You were brought to annual check-ups and were never neglected. I even allowed you to eat your weird diet, despite what the doctor said. I just wanted you to be happy. That's all I've ever wanted.

Andrei is growing into a beautiful child and another is nearly here. They're the next generation of Stones and we know they'll grow to appreciate how special this family truly is. I hope you do too.

Xx

Mother

After a couple of days of edits and deliberation, I reply:

I am sorry that my previous email left you feeling so attacked. I didn't mean to lash out at you or say you didn't do a good job. It seems you may have misconstrued my intentions, or I failed to state them well.

Of course you and Father did many wonderful things. I

know you gave up a lot to raise this family and how much we meant to you. I'm not sitting around wishing life dealt me a better hand. It frustrates me that you can't accept that I can have both gratitude and sadness. Like you said: no family is perfect. I don't expect ours to be. I just want to be able to express my feelings without being beaten down or banished for doing so—or told that I'm crazy.

We can't change the past. All we can do is decide how we want to be moving forward. But when past behaviors continue in present day, it's hard to feel we've gotten anywhere. I'm tired of being made out to be crazy and ungrateful. I am neither.

People look to you for approval. Each time you froze me out, not one person contacted me—not during holidays or birthdays or ever. I'm not sure you realize how much that hurts. Especially as an adoptee.

I love you and hope we can talk about these things and have a better relationship in the future.

Love,
Shay

I never hear from her again.

RECLAMATION

Through Dottie's network, I've started EMDR to help ease my trigger points. My therapist is Asian and she keeps forgetting I wasn't raised by Asian parents. It's a little bothersome at times but I otherwise trust her. She's smaller than I am and dresses like a '60s fashion icon. Being around someone so unafraid to be herself encourages me to do the same.

While there are several ways to practice EMDR, Ms. Chung uses a conductor's baton. She waves it widely from side to side. She asks, "What's coming up for you?" I blurt out whatever pops into mind and we take it from there. Sometimes it's hard for my eyes to follow while my brain is supposed to be free-flowing. But since it's proven to be great for people with C-PTSD, I figure it's worth a shot.

For Operation: Reclaim My Body, I've also signed up with a yoga studio. Standing in Warrior II and moving in sync with other women is where I am finding my power. I feel the energy move through my legs, up my core, and out through my fingertips. I already notice the difference when I'm walking in public. My shoulders are back and my chin's more upright.

One of the best things the Bay Area has to offer is the never ending selection of trails. Jae-Mee and I hike through hills, farms, redwoods, around lakes, coastal cliffs, through caves, across wooden bridges, along creeks and waterfalls.

There are bobcats and pelicans, foxes and so many vultures, ground squirrels, lizards and elk. It's amazing how dropping into new scenery has a way of making you feel you can be new.

At the peak of a trail on Tiburon, we stop and marvel over the panoramic bay. There's a view of the Golden Gate, Richmond Bridge, and Bay Bridge. There are sailboats, kite surfers, and ferries.

"This is amazing," I gasp.

With his arm around my back, Jae-Mee squeezes me closer. "And we live here."

I breathe deeply. "This is our home now, isn't it? We did it. We made life better."

"And to think there were so many days that I thought you wouldn't make it out of the hospital."

"Someday I'll make something good of that experience."

"How so?"

"I don't know but I've got to do something—help others somehow."

"That's admirable and all, but I think you've earned the right to just enjoy life for a while."

I've started initiating affection in bed. Sometimes I still struggle with knee-jerk reactions that cause physical pain for poor Jae-Mee, but we laugh it off together.

He says, "Just tell me when you want to stop. I won't be upset." And just knowing the option is there takes a lot of the edge off.

I'm actually beginning to enjoy sober sex. It's a whole new activity from the sex I used to know. And it doesn't at all resemble pita bread pizza.

I ask him later, as we're falling asleep, "All those times I put you off—before the hospital—did it make you want to leave? Tell me the truth."

"Sometimes. I didn't understand what was going on. I just figured you weren't attracted to me anymore. Guess it hurt my ego."

"What about after the hospital—all those months with no sex? Did you worry what you got yourself into?"

"I won't lie. It was hard to keep things in check sometimes."

"Did you ever think of leaving? But feel guilty, maybe?"

"Maybe for fleeting moments of frustration. But... I believed things would get better. And now they are."

"I'll make it up to you someday."

"That's not necessary. You were dealing with your own, much heavier shit. You don't owe people for treating you the way you deserve to be treated."

"Isn't that gratitude?" I wonder.

"Gratitude is painted all over your face when I watch you look at beautiful things. It's in your smile and the way you hum when you're making food. I don't need you to pay me back for staying with you. I'm here because I want to be."

And it's in this moment that I understand a piece of what Dottie was referring to when she said, know your worth.

Growing up, I was always hearing how grateful I should be. It never seemed I was showing it enough. I thought I owed everyone for trying and failing to love me. And when it failed, I believed it was because I didn't try hard enough, behave well enough, or somehow wasn't lovable. Somewhere, sewn into the fabric of my DNA, was the question of whether that was the true reason my birth mother and everyone else left me.

I fight off my instinct to tell Jae-Mee that I don't deserve him—because no one deserves anyone. Do they? I say nothing and squeeze his hand.

LIFE AND DEATH

How much can the heart love? Is it only as strong as we are brave? The more I allow my heart to fathom real love, the harder it aches—for all I haven't known, all that I have, and all that might be.

This morning I peed on three sticks that told me I'm pregnant. While it wasn't planned, I couldn't be happier. Knowing there's life growing inside my stomach—the part of my body that's given me the most trouble—feels incredible.

I lie down on the floor and feel like I'm floating. I imagine that's what it's like for some people when they find God. Suddenly I believe in a higher power and she lives inside me. I envision my body as a garden blooming to nourish this little being who will rule my world.

Because I'm not showing yet, I'm nervous when people unconsciously push past me in crowds. I flinch when someone runs a light as I cross the road. I'm accustomed to bracing myself for the inevitable whenever things appear to be going too well. I make a mental note to bring it into my next session with Ms. Chung.

I put the three tests in a bracelet box and wrap it with a nice bow. When Jae-Mee arrives home from work, I tell him, "Just a little something I thought you might like."

Pushing it back towards me he says, "Aw baby, I told

you—you don't owe me anything."

"Just open it," I insist, pushing it back towards him.

My heart jumps as he unties the bow. When he opens the lid, I watch his face quickly morph from confusion to elation. His mouth opens in silence a few beats before he says, "Holy shit."

We fall onto the bed and embrace giddily. I tell Jae-Mee that I just know it's a girl. We joke about naming her Pais-Lee II or other faux Korean names similar to his. I tell Jae-Mee I'd always wished my name matched my face better, the way his does. It could've bypassed so much confusion and disappointment. We talk about how we'll do the Doljanchi and maybe other cultural traditions. It's a euphoric few hours that I'll never forget.

Still riding the high while prepping dinner, I receive an urgent email to call my cousin Samantha. She knows we live in the Bay Area and understands that I'm not comfortable with anyone having my number—in part, to guard them from awkward situations.

She asks, "Have you seen the emails from your sister? Are you sitting down?"

I find my way to a chair on the balcony. "What's up?"

"Your father died," she says, just like that.

I say a hundred things but apparently none of them out loud.

Samantha asks, "Are you there? You okay?"

"Um," I release, to let her know I'm still on the line. "What happened?"

"He died this morning. I told Myra I'd find a way to get the message to you. She was awful to me. She doesn't believe that I don't have your number."

"Did she say how he died?"

"In his sleep. Your mother woke up and saw him. That's all I know."

"Oh. Well… thanks... for letting me know."

"What are you going to do, Shay?"

"I'm not sure," I tell her. "I've got to go now."

DAMNED

I'm not able to cry for him and that makes my chest swell with guilt and a sprinkling of anger. Somehow I imagined we'd have final words. I never thought we'd make peace with one another, but perhaps find peace from each other.

I open the family folder and skim through the latest.

Myra says: Daddy's dead! Don't you give a shit? How selfish of you to just cut out your family! Call me and tell me when you're coming home!

Ivan writes: Not that you care, but Father's gone and Mother's a wreck. Get your ass home and be the daughter she deserves.

Jack offers: Sorry to say this in an email but Father died. We miss you. Hope to see you back home for the funeral.

I'm suddenly reminded of the girl in the online KAD group with a similar conundrum—and all the feedback she received.

I set up a Skype call with Dottie. Her silver hair and gold-rimmed glasses bring me comfort. All that's missing is that white porcelain cat and the calming lavender scent in the air.

Without preface, I blurt out, "My father died."

"I'm sorry. This must be difficult for you."

"I feel kind of numb."

Dottie allows my silence to linger.

"They want me home for the funeral."

"Do you want to go?"

"I don't think so," I admit. "Is that unforgivable?"

"The only person who needs to accept your decision is you. How do you feel about not going?"

"I'm just afraid I'll be further blamed and misunderstood. It's not that I wouldn't want to be there if I felt it would do any good. But I'm not going to get any closure. And I honestly think they expect me to come running to continue playing make believe."

"Tell me more."

"No matter what I do, it won't be good enough. If I go, they'll tell me how awful I am for not being there for his final days. And if I don't, they'll tell me how rude and selfish I continue to be."

"Sounds like you know there's nothing you can do to gain their approval."

"And I don't want to listen to them carry on about what a wonderful man he was. I think I'd lose my mind for good. I can't do it. I just can't."

"You don't have to."

"But I feel like I do. They've demanded my return. No one asked. Jack's the only one who didn't pressure or guilt me directly. If I don't go, I'll never hear the end of it."

"Shay," Dottie pauses, collecting her thoughts. "You don't have to hear anything. They don't have your number. They don't know where you live. You've blocked them on social media. All they have is your email address—which you can change or continue to filter and ignore. Don't let them throw you off your rock. You still have control."

I take a deep breath and exhale through my nose.

"I'm pregnant. The test says eight weeks."

"Congratulations."

"I just… can't handle the stress of being back in that house with them and their madness. It won't be good for anyone."

"Sounds like you've made up your mind. Are you seeking my approval?"

"I think I just needed to talk it out. But what if I change my mind and decide to go anyway?"

"Whatever you decide is fine—so long as you're doing what you think is right for you."

"I'm finally happy and moving on. I've worked so hard to get here. I'm afraid of ending up back at square one."

"You're in control. Hold onto it."

IF I DO

I know exactly what I want to say. I spend an hour crafting the email to send to the family. I pick out the floral arrangement. Everything is set to go. And then I change my mind.

There are good reasons for me not to go. But in the end, it just doesn't feel right. I don't want to hold a grudge. It doesn't mean I have to stay at the house or spend time with the family. I can just show up for the burial and leave.

Jae-Mee comes along for support. One of his coworkers offers to take care of Paisley. We book our flights and a room for two nights in Harvard Square. I send a brief email to Myra, Ivan, and Jack, to let them know we'll be there.

While we're waiting at the gate, my stomach pains return with a vengeance. I hear myself yelp as I keel over.

Jae-Mee's alarmed at the sight of me. "What's wrong?"

"It's just… the usual, I'm sure."

He unscrews the cap on his water and hands it to me. I shake my head, burying my face in my thighs.

"Do you want me to see if there's a medic on site?" he asks, peering around. "Someone should be able to help."

"It's okay," I moan. I practice my meditative breath exercises. "I just need to sit here a moment."

Jae-Mee panics and blurts, "We shouldn't have come. I didn't want to tell you what to do, but I had a bad feeling about this."

"Jae-Mee, please," I beg, continuing my breathing.

"They always find a way to get to you," he says. "They're evil, fucked up people."

"Enough!" I snap. "I just can't…"

He paces until he calms down. "I'm sorry. What can I do?"

"Just please… I need quiet. Okay?"

We sit in silence while others pretend not to look.

The pain is so bad that I can't hold back moans of anguish. The subsequent embarrassment only compounds my pain.

A voice in my head says, Relax. Breathe. It's okay. Breathe in. Breathe out. Let it flow. It will pass. Pretty soon it'll all be over. Good girl. That's my girl.

I start to make my way to the restroom, afraid I might vomit.

Jae-Mee cries out, "Shay!"

I turn and follow his eyes to the seat that's covered in blood.

I rush to the restroom while Jae-Mee grabs our things and trails behind me. He waits outside the door.

I burst through the extra-large stall for wheelchairs and mothers. My hands shake trying to lock it. I pull down my pants and collapse on the toilet. My stomach convulses as I lean forward, stifling my voice. When I dare look, I pass out. I come to when my head hits the toilet paper holder.

My baby. She's gone. I never got a chance to meet her. Out of three generations, why am I the one here, alone, again?

I try to clean myself up but it's of little use. I need a change of clothes.

Jae-Mee calls to me. "Are you okay?"

"No," I whimper.

"Shay?" he calls, more urgently.

"No!" I bellow.

"I'm coming in."

I open the stall door. He rushes in with our things.

"She's gone," I cry. "I lost her."

"Are you sure?"

I nod and, while I'm still on the toilet, he holds me as we sob together for what feels like an eternity.

"Here. Let's get you changed," he says, softly. Unzipping my case, he pulls out underwear and clean pants. "I'll be right back."

When Jae-Mee returns with his hands full of wet and dry paper towels, I ask, "Can you do me a favor?"

"Anything," he whispers.

"Go and get some kind of jar—a bottled drink and wash it out. I want to take what's left of her with me." While I know how crazy it all must seem, I need to do this.

"Um… I don't know if," he tries. "I'm not…"

"Please," I plead.

When he returns, I'm dressed and nearly ready to go. He turns around when I scoop up what I can and secure the lid.

"I know how this looks," I confess. "And that scientifically—"

"Do what you've gotta do," he whispers.

BEYOND BELIEF

On the ride home, I call the doctor's office for an emergency drop-in. We confirm that our baby is truly gone. The rest of the appointment is a blur.

I send an email to Myra:

I'm sad to report that we're not heading home after all. At the airport, I miscarried our child. Please let the others know not to expect me.

Ten minutes later, I receive a response:

I'm sorry you can't get your priorities right. That's too bad about the baby, but I truly believe God has plans for us and everything happens for a reason. Maybe you weren't ready to be a mother since you can't even be a good daughter? In any case, it's still pretty selfish and shitty that you can't be here for the rest of us. You've known your father for practically your whole life. He did so much for you. The baby wasn't even a person yet. I'll be sure to let everyone know. But you'll live to regret this.

Enraged, I write back a succinct:

FUCK. YOU.

I place the email filter back on and turn off my phone.

I scream as loud as I can into a pillow—maybe nine or ten times.

Jae-Mee sends flowers to the funeral home. "They won't be satisfied but at least we'll know we did the right thing."

We stay in bed all weekend—crying, holding onto each other out of desperation, and watching mindless TV.

When Jae-Mee heads to work on Monday, he says, "You should really get out of the house if you can. Maybe go across the street to the beach. Some fresh air might help."

Forcing myself up and out, I float in the bay and sleep in the sun. I let my mind wander without trying to make sense or organize anything in it.

I watch a family playing in the sand, burying who I assume to be the father.

A voice in my head says, "My father is buried."

I picture Mother floating up in the sky with Myra, Ivan, and Jack holding onto her red ribbons—like a big inflated parade float.

The next generation of Stones will likely hear what a saint our father was. In some ways, his legacy will be true—but that won't make it honest.

I used to think Father was a simple man but that's because I hardly knew him. I don't think he was so simple anymore. I don't think anyone really is. It's just a matter of how much they're willing and able to share.

Mother had one sister. We don't know if she's dead or alive. They either fought or were estranged for as far back as I recall. I used to always take Mother's side when she'd ramble on about how awful her sister was. Now I gather there's more to the story.

Nobody's pure evil and nobody's godly. We're all a jumbled up mess of good and bad.

I think back to how important it was for me to make Mother proud and to pay her and Father back. I consider the danger I put myself in, trying to get noticed at the recording studio. I wanted them to think I was a good investment. I wanted to feel approved of and loved. I wanted to make them proud; to repay them for saving my life. I didn't want to keep owing them so much.

Now I think it's a pretty shitty thing to make an adopted child feel indebted.

All that time catatonic—as terrible as it was, it was somewhat familiar. With the Stones, I could never be heard or seen beyond the surface. I had to fall so deep into my subconscious in order to find the truth.

In Mother's last letter, she said they never chose me—we were matched at random. It was as simple as that, despite it differing greatly from the story she used to tell me as a child. She said God knew what he was doing when he brought us together. No wonder I always found it hard to believe in him.

After spending all this time trying to find who I am, I finally know what I believe:

- I believe Mother wasn't magic but she was a magician. She manipulated her audience and could make you disappear.
- I believe in Jae-Mee and actionable love.
- I believe in the truth—and facing it as soon as you're able.
- I believe in the balance of things.
- I believe no one owes anyone their suffering, happiness, or anything in between.

- I believe the good we get is a gift to be cherished.
- I believe there's still hope for most of us.
- I believe in myself.
- I believe that I'm capable, sane, and honest.
- I believe I was raised among rocks but I'm not made of Stone.
- I believe in keurium, and that I'll always ache from the deep longing I have for so many people, memories, and places—some of which were never real.
- But mostly, I believe that it's time to live free from those who can't help but hurt me.

EXHILARATION

Resting on the parking block of our designated space, I rise to stand as the car pulls in. Jae-Mee's brows lift as I hop into the passenger seat.

"Can we just drive for a bit?"

Putting the car in reverse, he says, "Sure. Why not?" And I love him all the more for it.

We drive aimlessly across the island. I gaze up at the long, skinny trunks of palm trees and back down to the colorful bungalows. We pass people of all ages, colors, and status—on bicycles, skateboards, and foot. They seem happy.

I think, we live in an urban paradise. Why aren't we all happy?

And then I remember.

When we reach the Posey Tube, I unroll my window and stick my head out. At the top of my lungs, I shout into the echoing tunnel, "Mo-ther-fuck-ing hell!" dragging each syllable out to my satisfaction.

Jae-Mee unrolls his window and screams, "Yeah! What she said!"

I cackle and holler, "What the fuck is wrong with everybody? Why does everyone suck?"

Jae-Mee tilts his head sideways and shouts, "I know! What the fuck, people?"

When we reach the end of the tunnel and emerge into sunshine we close our windows, amused with ourselves. Tears are squirting out of my eyes. My stomach cramps. I can't remember when I last felt so good.

Driving through Oakland, each time we approach an overpass, our windows glide back down. We carry on, shouting, "My family's fucking crazy!" and "Seriously! Her family's fucking nuts!" Eventually, we move on to swirling sirens and animal sounds.

I tell Jae-Mee, "This is the most fun I've had in years!"

"We're just getting started, baby!"

We go on a tear.

We hit the driving range in Montclair and whack the paint clean off a hundred golf balls, sipping beer and laughing maniacally at nothing.

We grab a couple of drinks down at Heinold's First and Last Chance in Jack London Square. It's hard to tell if we're getting as tipsy as it seems, or if it's just the crazy uneven floor.

Across the way at Plank, we eat fries, guzzle more booze, and make an embarrassing show of corn hole and bocce. We find it hysterical, of course, and realize we've had more than enough to drink. Regardless, we stumble up the road to The Night Light for one fancy drink each.

Leaving the car in a garage, we catch the ferry back to Alameda for some mouthwatering Burmese food. At this point, our communication is pared down to slurred fragments and unappetizing groans of food appreciation.

I come to as the Lyft driver slows down in front of our place on Shoreline Drive. Jae-Mee helps me out of the backseat and we make our wobbly way up the stairs and into our safe, cozy home.

Waking up the next morning in last night's clothes reminds

me of my early twenties, but without the guilt. I feed Paisley and crack open a bottle of kombucha, bringing it back to bed.

"Ouch," moans Jae-Mee, still in his clothes, too. "Why must no good deed go unpunished?"

Patting his side, I tell him, "I needed that. Thanks for blowing off some steam with me." I lean over to kiss his temple.

"My pleasure," he mumbles into the pillow. "We should do it more often."

"Yes. But not today."

"We're out of practice," he grunts.

He reaches his hand over to find me and flops it down on my thigh. I drop a hand on top of his. "I almost feel like a normal person today."

With a little more life in him, Jae-Mee says, "Please never be normal." He pulls me closer.

Resting on his shoulder, I mumble, "I don't think you have to worry about that."

There's a warm glow radiating in the center of my chest. "Maybe the worst of everything is over now? Maybe the second half of life will make up for the first?"

Squeezing my hand, he says, "Could be."

It feels good to pretend all my hardships are behind me— even if just for the moment. There's no harm in a few beats of temporary bliss.

JANG-MI

I've chosen a way to honor her.

At a plant nursery in Berkeley, I ask for Rose of Sharon seedlings—Korea's national flower. We select a planter box and set it up on the balcony at home. Atop a thick layer of soil, I distribute the remnants of what would've been our child. I cover it with another layer of soil and the seedlings are planted above it.

"There. Now we can watch her grow."

Jae-Mee squeezes my hand. "Jang-Mi."

"What's that?"

"Rose."

The sun warms my face as I repeat, "Jang-Mi."

We sit, eyes fixed on the seedlings as if they might blossom before our eyes. I stay out on the balcony all day and well into the night. Jae-Mee never coaxes me to come in. He fixes us snacks and cocktails and strums the guitar quietly to my right.

The next morning in bed, I tell him, "We'll try again," and he nods sleepily.

Since the miscarriage, I've been charting my cycle in a fertility app. I take my temperature at the same time every morning and input any noteworthy details.

My doctor suggests I see an acupuncturist and take multiple supplements. She says my charts are all over the place but it's normal for women post-miscarriage. I tell her that my period has always been irregular—which is why I didn't test until I was eight weeks. When I ask why I need extra help if it's normal, she says, "You're older now. We call it Advanced Maternal Age. Your numbers are okay but time's not on your side."

On a walk along the coast of Bay Farm Island, I ask Jae-Mee, "What if Jang-Mi was our only chance at a biological connection?"

"We weren't even trying. Why wouldn't it happen again?"

"The doctor said pregnancy after 35 is referred to as 'Advanced Maternal Age'—which replaced an even worse term, 'Geriatric Pregnancy.'"

Jae-Mee says, point-blank, "She sucks. Get a new doctor. Who needs that attitude?"

"She's just stating the facts."

"Then give it some time. We're just starting. These days you hear of women having kids well into their forties. You're not even thirty-eight."

I turn my head to the waves moving in the bay. "You're right. I need to relax. It's just that there's so much to learn. I didn't know about follicular and luteal phases, basal body temperatures, LH hormones..."

He stops, leaning on one hip, and says, "We conceived Jang-Mi. Do what you think is best, but maybe don't worry so much."

"Easy for you to say."

Every morning, I go through the routine of temping, inputting data, swallowing supplements, and meticulously analyzing my chart. For one week each cycle, I test my urine for signs of ovulation. Two weeks later, I test my urine for pregnancy. A couple of months down the road, I begin weekly acupuncture appointments and mix Chinese herbs twice daily. Sex begins to ease back into pita bread pizza territory. It's hard to keep it fresh when you're doing it non-stop, and you feel like a couple of failures.

When I try to relax, I keep hearing my doctor say, "Time is not on your side."

When I'm scrolling Facebook, I'm flooded with photos of my adoptee network's newborns, and stories of how much their children are healing their wounds. Through stubborn tears, I read what it's like for adoptees to finally see their own features reflected back at them. I wonder if I'll ever be lucky enough to know how that feels.

I dream about how Jang-Mi might have looked had she made it all the way through. Would she have had my eyes or might she have been blessed with Jae-Mee's subtle double-lids? Would she have dark brown waves or Jae-Mee's slick, black strands? Would she have become short and sturdy like me, or might she have grown to be long and thin like her father?

Sometimes I sit outside near her planter and talk as if there's a soul in there waiting for the comforting sound of my voice—the way only a fetus-carrying mother's can be. I tell her, "It's a shame you never got to see how beautiful it is here. I would've shown you all the best places I've found. You would've had such a great dad."

Other times I speak to her as if being cheated from this life transported her into some magical, all-knowing realm. She's become a god to me.

If you've lived a life like mine, you might understand the deep desire to believe in something bigger than you—paired with the deeper skepticism of it. It's like wanting to light a candle with the fear of fire.

SKIN ON SKIN

When you've been trying a while to get pregnant, time moves like honey through a cocktail straw. It's an exercise of waiting—to see patterns, to know when to have sex, when to test—for that Holy Shit Moment to come again so you can wait to make sure it will keep.

There are a few weeks of trying to be hopeful followed by another two weeks of resenting my body. I slip back down into Law of Attraction guilt, wondering if maybe it's not happening because I didn't visualize it well or want it badly enough. Some say if you don't believe it can happen it won't.

I fight off the taunting question of whether Mother was right—that I'm not cut out to be a mother.

I ask my acupuncturist, "Could I be sabotaging this with my fears?"

"Maybe if you're stressing yourself out."

"Are we to blame for our stress? Is it ever the fault of whatever's causing it?"

"There's no point in placing blame. It's our responsibility to handle whatever comes our way." She inserts the final needle and tells me, "Try to relax. Fall asleep if you can."

I thank her and omit the fact that I can't fall asleep with sixteen needles in me. Yes, I was counting. I try not to worry that my body will convulse and accidentally push a needle in too far, or that I'll fall right off the damn table, needles lost inside me forever. I suppose it's as relaxing as attempting savasana on a wire above Times Square might be. You'd have to reach a level of zen that I haven't mastered.

In some ways, the needles feel like Ivan's and Myra's words stabbing into me. And maybe that's why I had that dream about the children in that cave. Maybe they were the children and that woman who controlled them was Mother.

Acupuncture eventually gets better. On the sixth or seventh appointment, something amazing happens. I enter a state of calm that leads somewhere new. I see myself in a large, round tub holding a newborn to my chest as I sob freely. In real life, my tears are never free. I fight them and they sometimes win. But in this dream state, I feel it as if it is real. Holding warm, soft flesh from my own to my own, I want to stay but the intensity of it all wakes me, returning me to the dimmed room. I hear the familiar audio track of a babbling brook that always makes me think I need to urinate. I notice the subtle tear on the corner of the mauve floral print on the wall.

The acupuncturist knocks on the door and enters with a hushed, "Hey there. Feeling relaxed?"

I don't know how to verbalize what I'm feeling so I simplify it with, "I think I got to a good place this time."

Walking back to the apartment, my body doesn't seem real. I've still got one foot in the imaginary world I'd just left. It almost feels like I'm walking home to see my baby; to hold him or her close to my heart. But when I open the door, Paisley greets me and I say, "It's just us girls here, eh?"

"Meow."

I sit down at my desk and try to finish a logo project but my head's just not in it. It's hard to focus on bicycles when all I want to do is go back to that place where I held my newborn child. With each passing minute, it seems more like a dream. I don't want to let it get away from me.

It's seventy-two degrees in Alameda. The sun lights up our balcony in the afternoon. I water Jang-Mi and rest beside her on the chair with my feet pressed against the railing. Paisley sits on my lap and I pat her black fur that's warmed and auburn-tinted from the sun.

I wonder about family and what that word means. The more I think about it, the less I understand. As a child, I accepted that it meant whatever I was told. Family was not always blood. Family was a group of people living together whether they liked it or not. Family was all I'd ever have.

Family went from being all I had to the only thing that I don't. Most days, I'm happier. I know myself better. I like myself better. But I still want to understand what it means to be a family. I want to have my own family—I think.

And then I'm struck with a shocking possibility: I may be sabotaging pregnancy because my body can't believe I want something that I don't fully understand. I can fool my mind but I can't fool my body. It always knows.

My stomach starts to ache. That feeling of being zapped by a cattle prod overcomes me. I try to hold still, as movement amplifies pain. I take slow shallow breaths. Paisley reaches a paw to my chin but I let my head fall back, closing my eyes.

I must've passed out from the pain because I wake when Jae-Mee calls my name. He kisses me and asks, "What's wrong?"

"Just my stomach," I whisper. "It'll pass."

Bouncing his knee, he says, "There's got to be something we can do about this. You've had this—what?—most of your life? Maybe it's time to take it more seriously."

"This whole trying to get pregnant thing is stressful."

"Maybe we should stop for a while?"

"We don't have time. I'll find better ways to manage my stress."

He sighs. "Well, if it gets worse, we'll have to make some decisions. I don't like seeing you in pain all the time. Nothing's worth that."

In that moment, I realize I'll need to start concealing my pain.

I want to tell Jae-Mee what I saw in my acupuncture appointment, but it hurts too much to talk. So I close my eyes and try to return to that moment and make it feel real again. Maybe then, it'll happen.

A GIFT FROM THE GRAVE

My eyes pop open to the dark room. Jae-Mee's chest rises and falls beside me. I sharpen my eyes on the outline of the curtains and spot Paisley's silhouette at the foot of the bed.

Tick tick tick tick tick tick.

I jolt up and turn my head slowly, trying to discern where the sound is coming from.

Am I awake? Or am I caught in this nightmare again?

Carefully slipping out of the covers, so as not to wake Jae-Mee, I tiptoe towards the dresser. Tilting my ear down to it, I don't hear anything, but open the top drawer anyway.

Tick tick tick tick tick.

I pinch myself twice.

Tick tick.

I'm spun in another direction. Using the light from my phone to creep around like a burglar, I press my ear into closets and cabinets.

TICK TICK TICK.

On the kitchen cart, beneath a pile of circulars and junk mail, I find a small package addressed to me from an office in Boston. Pressing it to my ear, the ticks are deafening. I tear it open to find a gold pocket watch and a letter that reads:

Yes, I tracked you down since you can't be bothered to

communicate with the family who kept you alive and gave you everything. Don't worry. I have no desire to come out and see you and neither does anyone else. I'm simply honoring Daddy's wishes. He wanted you to have this. I also thought you should know the truth. Daddy never laid a finger on you. You were the untouchable Asian princess, don't you know? He looked at you with nothing but awe and admiration but you were off-limits. So maybe he came into your room and watched you sometimes. Maybe he was a little unorthodox with how he showed his affection. But he did nothing wrong. He was a good man. He confided in me because he knew I understood and loved him like no other. No matter what he did for you, you denied him love—right up to the very end. Now that's yours to live with. Too late to change.

Our family is getting on just fine without you, but I'll never forgive you for all the pain you've caused us. I hope you rot in hell.

I collapse on the floor with my back up against the cupboards, shaking with the package and letter in my hands. I drop the pocket watch on the floor. I shiver as my eyes fall upon its gold casing. My hands don't dare hold it. I'm afraid to connect to the many moments I'd erased from my mind.

My heart pounds through my chest like terror banging down the door it's locked behind. Suddenly I know: The ticks weren't just from the parlor clock.

I see my toddler hands holding onto the pocket watch, rubbing my fingers over the grooves of the engraved emblem. I was mesmerized by the second hand's revolution. Father knew it would make me feel special to have access to his beloved watch on a chain. He brought it to me as a treat sometimes when the rest of the house was asleep.

Confused and enraged, I wonder if Father told Myra he never touched me to make her feel special, too?

Tears roll down my face and splash onto the letter. After a weak crumple, I toss it and kick it aside. I'm bawling my eyes out, pulsing in silence. My breath empties out so completely that I gasp for air.

I feel like a house broken into once more. I'm so angry. And I'm annoyed to be so heartbroken for Myra because she defends him and I'm sure it's the best she can do. Her commitment to his sainthood is stronger than her commitment to her own sanity.

I understand how it's easier for her to throw me away than to upset the fantasy of our past. And I get it. I suppose if I weren't adopted—or if I'd ever felt loved—it would've been harder to leave.

He never touched you. You were the untouchable Asian princess, I hear her voice say.

He lied.

I detect jealousy in her wording. I wonder if that somehow played into the changes she made to her appearance. Was she running away from that broken girl? Did she subconsciously blame it all on her looks? Did she hate me for being untouched—according to him? Is that why she's always been cruel about my being Asian and adopted?

All those years wishing I looked more like her and Mother, was she wishing she looked more like me because she thought it could've kept her safe?

And if he never touched me, why would my mind concoct it? Did I need an ugly enough reason to leave since Mother's abuse was more covert?

No. If anything, the gold pocket watch solidifies the awful truth. I shove it with the letter into the fridge because it's on my way back to bed. And clearly, I've lost my mind.

I slide back under the covers. I lie awake singing Madonna's "Live to Tell" in my head on repeat.

HUMAN

When Jae-Mee opens his eyes, it's like I've been waiting ten years to ask him, "Why didn't you tell me I got a package?"

"What?" Stretching his long body, he moans and rolls to his side.

Growing impatient, I tell him, "I found the package."

"Oh. Right," he says, rubbing his eyes. "I must've forgot. Why? Was it important?"

"It was from Myra and Father."

"I figured it was something from Amazon."

"She tracked me down. I told you—they always find a way."

"What was it? A bomb?"

"Not funny. But yeah, kind of."

"Sorry. I'm still waking up."

"It's a fucking pocket watch. And the letter—you'll have to read for yourself." I shiver.

"Do I have to? I'm tired of their drama. I thought moving out here meant putting them behind us."

His comment catches me off-guard. I retract and turn cold. Words can't express how I feel, so I lie there in silence. Jae-Mee touches my arm and I pull it away.

"Please don't be like that," he begs.

I'm stubbornly fighting back tears and feeling more alone

than ever.

He heads for the bathroom. When I hear the shower running, I get up, make myself a cup of tea and take it out to the balcony.

Sitting alongside Jang-Mi, I think, maybe I'm being selfish and needy. It's not like I wanted this. Life's been difficult enough with the miscarriage and failing to make another baby. This is the last thing I need. Am I supposed to ignore it? Not tell him about the major happenings in my life simply because he's tired of it? I'm tired of it, too. But I don't get to be done with it just because it's what I want.

I sulk, eyes fixed on the blue waves, the dogs, and their people. I wonder what it's like to be normal, or at least more normal than this.

I hear Jae-Mee padding around inside. He opens the refrigerator door and I suddenly remember shoving the package in there. The door closes and I hear paper rattling. I'm not sure if he's reading the letter or putting it aside. I'm afraid to look.

He pops his head out the door and asks, "Hungry?"

Feeling further denied, I shrug. He groans and disappears.

A storm's brewing inside me. I head inside to grab my keys and a hat. My eyes catch the pocket watch on the counter. Jae-Mee must've taken it out of the fridge. I grab and drop it into my pocket. As I open the door to leave, I hear him ask, "Where are you—" but I shut the door behind me and carry on.

Stomping along the beach, I try hard to conceal my inner rage but it's uncontainable. I throw the pocket watch as far as I can into the bay. I kick seaweed, spinning off-balance, and fall to the sand. My arms drop to my thighs as I scream into my hands. I wipe the tears and snot from my face but feel it cling to my hair.

I can't blame Jae-Mee for wanting to move on. He's been patient, dealing with the effects of my traumas without many complaints. But they are my traumas and I never asked for them. The way he acted this morning sparked my insecurity about being a burden. It awakened a pain buried since my youth—always feeling sorry for how the bad things that happen to me impact and inconvenience others.

In my head, I scream to Myra: I'm sorry you felt I was protected by my foreign skin. But I wasn't.

In my head, I scream louder: I'm not sorry. I have nothing to be sorry for. Your pain is not greater than mine. You weren't more entitled to safety and love, simply because you were born into the family. And you didn't deserve a good father any more than I did.

I shout at Mother: Your husband abused your girls and you let him. Did you feel we deserved to be damaged for causing his eyes to stray? Did you think I'd never grow to see who and what you really are? Did you actually believe you could keep us all under your thumb forever with your lies and manipulation? Someday, the rest of them will see. It may be on your deathbed—or theirs—but they'll see.

I scream at Father: How long had you planned to send me the pocket watch? Did you want me to completely unravel? Surely you knew how it would affect me—like one final clutch to my heart from the grave.

Those who pass me are obviously unnerved. I pull my hat down a notch. I slow down my breathing, trying to pull myself together, suddenly aware of the mess I've been.

Miles from home, I find a tree and tuck myself behind it. I lean against it, pull my legs up against my chest and rest my arms on my knees. I close my eyes.

I wake to a dark sky. A jolt of panic strikes my heart. I stand up and stumble a few paces, trying to make sense of where I am and remember what happened.

I walk in the direction I believe home to be. With the sun down, there's a chill in the air. I hadn't grabbed a sweater or jacket, not realizing how long I'd be gone. Hugging myself for warmth, I walk until things start to look familiar.

It's a quarter past nine when I walk through the door. Paisley greets me with figure-eights around my shoes. Jae-Mee's not home. In the bedroom, I find my phone with two missed calls and a message. Jae-Mee says, "Shit. You left your phone here. If you get back and I'm gone, let me know you're okay. Please?"

As I'm about to call, he walks through the door. I drop the phone on the bed and head towards him. He throws his arms around me and weeps. "I'm so sorry."

"It's okay."

"No it's not. I read the letter. I can't imagine what's been going through your head."

"I'm fine now," I assure him.

"Well, you shouldn't be. Your family…" He shakes his head. "I fucked up big time."

"It struck a bad nerve. I felt like an imposition—how I felt in my family."

"I'm really sorry. I was worried the letter and my shitty reaction pushed you over the edge. What's the deal with the pocket watch?"

"I'll tell you later. Okay? I'm just spent."

"Alright. Where'd you go?"

"I walked the beach—found a tree and passed out behind it." I shrug and inhale. "Look… I know this hasn't been easy on you, either. It's wrong of me to expect you to always put your emotions behind mine."

"It's human—after all you've been through."

"Well, you're human too. Sucks to be human. Am I right?" I twist my face into a silly expression, meant to lighten the mood.

"Fucking right," he says, running fingers through his hair.

THE TROUBLE WITH SURVIVORS

Show me the switch to flip from HURT to HEALED.

I want to live out those memes that refer to warrior women who are strong because of their pasts. Scratch that. I want to be strong in spite of my past. What caused my suffering deserves no credit. I'm bored with acknowledging it. I want to morph into this shiny new woman who's okay without having a mother or child.

The cruelest part about being a survivor is that knowing what you went through is not even close to half the battle. This "half the battle" fib is to coax you into making it that far. Don't get me wrong—it's a major achievement. But what they don't tell you is that with each level of healing, a new battle begins.

Buddhists claim: Life is suffering.

I'm not down with that. I want life to be love and laughter and art with a dose of realism commensurate with past suffering—which I feel must've hit its quota.

There are several potential friendships I've encountered at yoga and on freelance jobs, but I've stunted their growth. Innocent questions cause me to retract. There's a lightness to normal, healthy people that feels wrong to weigh down with the kind of honesty required for true connection when you're recovering from trauma.

Making friends with fellow survivors is also tricky. It begins with oversharing and perhaps too much blind compassion. We connect with the broken parts we see reflected, sometimes missing the context of the whole person.

There's also this term called "fleas" that's used to explain how survivors often display traits similar to the toxic people in our lives. Once we become aware of the toxic people we move on from, we notice these fleas on ourselves and others. Hopefully, the goal is to rid ourselves of them. I've noticed a few on me: the need to appear better than I am; and extreme reactions to situations in which I feel wronged. I'm working on their extermination. But sometimes seeing fleas on others can stab all your wounds. It's hard to witness the Stones' traits in others. It makes me want to run fast and far.

I understand that when you're held back and pushed down for so long, there can be the tendency to bounce full-force in the opposite direction once freed—like a slingshot effect. One woman in particular was always posting flamboyant selfies. She reminded me of Myra. She bragged about her accomplishments multiple times a day, but always accompanied by subtle put-downs to others. While I was happy to see another survivor push beyond the negativity of her past to repair her self-esteem, it still triggered certain feelings I thought I'd healed. And I didn't believe in her sincerity. Watching her was like watching a hot rod on the highway spinning wildly out of control while others cheered on, not cognizant of the danger. I couldn't help but guess how vulnerable she must have felt to need all of that approval.

It wasn't long before we heard she committed suicide. None of us knew how to process her death. The group moderators weren't trained professionals, so there was an array of uncomfortable responses in lieu of proper therapy.

Many of us were under- or unemployed, without health insurance, or living in precarious situations. Whether supplementing therapy sessions, or standing in for them, these online groups were the best most of us could get.

Another difficult aspect of being in these groups was the common wish to have been adopted. A few times I chimed in to explain that adoption doesn't guarantee a more loving or healthy family, and comes with many issues of its own. I shared my experiences, articles, and stats about adoptee suicide. But it's tiring trying to educate those clinging to their own fantasies.

I was about to leave the survivor groups, but then along came Jane. A lot of what she shared resonated. I appreciated the way she expressed her struggles and valued her much-needed wit in hard moments. I frequently commented with heartfelt words and she did the same.

Sometimes she'd inbox me to further the conversation in private. We seemed to share similar emotional reactions to much of the content in that group. A few nights I stayed up late, sipping wine, chatting away with her like old friends after Jae-Mee had fallen asleep. We talked about what we loved and hated about books and movies that showed child abuse, and how they always messed up the ending to appeal to the masses' need to believe that in the end, all is always forgiven.

Our budding friendship carried on for several months. Eventually, we discussed how cool it'd be to meet up in Vegas for a survivor's weekend.

I was excited when Jane took the next step to befriend me outside of the group. It meant she was no longer a fringe acquaintance reserved for recovery. She was the first new friend in my life away from the Stones. There was a remarkable feeling in creating promising bonds after severing so many that were dysfunctional.

And then her non-survivor posts began making their way into my feed. I had to do a double-take on the first one—an article share about immigrants taking away from the hardworking white people in the country. I clicked to see if it was satire but nope. Further dialog with others depicted a woman with a lot of misguided anger.

There were many more troubling posts, but the one that clinched it for me was a direct rant against blacks and other people of color. I quickly employed the block button. But it took some time to stop reeling from the shock of it all.

I checked my profile picture and although I had sunglasses on in my current photo, the one before it showed my Asian face in full bloom. I wasn't sure if she hadn't realized I was Asian, given my sunglasses and last name—or if I was a mere exception. While there's a perverse feeling of acceptance to be liked beyond one's usual tolerance, I'm no longer okay with being anyone's exception. Those who are don't realize they're basically giving permission to these people to claim they're not racist.

What I love about where we are in California is that Jae-Mee and I don't stick out everywhere like we used to. Our apartment complex and neighborhood is the first I've lived in that isn't at least 90% white. If anything, white people are outnumbered by people of color. When you're blended to this extent, it's easier to accept that there is no default. I don't think I realized until we moved here just how much Boston's segregation and casual racism impacted my personal views on what's okay and what's not.

And while there are unfortunate sides to being in self-moderated support groups, they've also been invaluable. To learn about the array of illnesses and disorders that contribute to abusive behavior is helping me take my pain less personally. Just like with my Korean Adoptee community, conversing with others with similar experiences helps me feel less alone.

BAPTISM

Beyond the traumatic reruns in your brain, the sleepless nights, and the facade of normalcy that you lose once you awaken and remove yourself from harm, there is freedom. Lying in the sun on the beach across from home, I ruminate on the child I once was, staring up at the sky, afraid to dream.

Being a rescue, gratitude is often instilled in you the way belonging is instilled in many biological children. To dream was to be ungrateful. Wanting more of anything equated to a selfishness so ugly, it'd bring shame on myself and everyone with the misfortune of knowing me. I believe many adoptees felt this way—and the damage is compounded when the ones you're to feel grateful for are the ones who are causing you harm.

I have to learn to accept the fact that both mothers left me. The first left when I had physical needs, and the second when I had emotional needs. It doesn't mean everyone will leave. But I do fear something will happen to Jae-Mee, more often than I should.

I open my eyes to the clear blue sky. Lifting my head, I peer out at the kids splashing about with their parents. I hold so much hope for them and their futures. And I see for the first time just how young and vulnerable I was when my traumas began.

I take a small hit from my vaporizer pen. CBD with low THC is meant to have healing properties for both body and mind. It's a new thing I'm trying.

I inhale the salty air. In my head a voice speaks. You are here. Really here. This is where you live. This is your new life. You may not have a child but you still have so much. Maybe you're to live firsthand some of the life you wished for Jang-Mi? Maybe you can fully allow yourself to be loved and feel loved? Maybe, while so much of life feels lost, there's more that you can't yet imagine?

Rising up from the sand, I walk steadfastly into the water. A flock of pelicans, stretched long and flat, soar inches from the gentle waves rolling onto the shore. I admire their uniformity. I wonder if they realize their sense of belonging or take it for granted.

I walk through salt water for what seems like miles before I give in and lie back to float. Although the water is warm, I shiver from the quick submergence.

I hold my breath before letting myself sink, sitting cross-legged on the seabed. Slowly exhaling bubbles through my nose, I wave my arms to stay down. Pressure builds in my head and lungs. When I emerge, I have an epiphany: It's time to change my name.

Back on shore, the salt water drying in the sun makes my skin tingle. I recall the name I was given as an infant: Song Na Ri. It likely meant nothing, decided by the orphanage or adoption agency to forge the necessary paperwork to sell me. But it was mine before I became Shay Nari Stone—my Korean identity trapped between who the Stones wanted me to be.

I no longer want to walk through life with my father's name. I want my name to match my face so there's no further awkward confusion. I don't want to continue being asked if Stone is my husband's name, or to feel forced into conversations about my uncomfortable past with strangers who are interested in the feel-good propaganda of adoption.

At dinner, Jae-Mee has a devilish grin. "You could take my name."

I scoff and roll my eyes. "That's romantic."

He smirks. "Don't worry. I'd ask you properly."

"Well, that'll be a day to remember. But regardless, I'm not taking your name."

His brows lift and he cocks his head a little. It's not the reaction he was hoping for.

"I don't mean to be rude. I want to create an identity that feels like my own. I've spent my whole life with someone else's."

Jae-Mee nods. "That's one of the sexiest things I've ever heard."

I toy with the idea of ditching my whole name, but decide to keep my first. I don't care for it, but it somehow feels wrong to erase it. Like it or not, Shay is also who I've been. Shay Nari Song more accurately represents who I am.

I download the forms and file them with the court. It will take several months to become recognized legally, but just starting the process to become my whole self is empowering.

"This is how it's done," a voice in my head speaks.

And there, as I'm walking down the court steps, I acknowledge that the voice in my head no longer sounds like anyone's but my own.

UNCERTAINTIES

Everyone on Team Shay has got a different idea. My gynecologist suggests harvesting eggs for IVF. It includes hormonal treatment—which threatens my emotional balance. My EMDR therapist wants me to go deeper into my trauma, but that kind of emotional stress seems counterproductive for baby making. Dottie thinks my body still needs time to heal, as traumatic realizations and the miscarriage are still fairly recent. She says chronic illness is common among survivors of child abuse. And my fertility acupuncturist thinks I have endometriosis—which could explain my erratic cycles and basal body temperatures, chronic pain, and possible infertility.

My gynecologist agrees that endometriosis is likely, but only diagnosed by surgery. I tell her, "But we already conceived once."

"Pregnancy can still happen for some but sometimes the disease gets in the way. I recommend a lap, for starters."

"A lap?"

"Laparoscopic surgery. It's a small incision to explore the pelvis and stomach—wherever the pain occurs. If they find it, they can try to remove some of it. You'll need to follow up with excision surgery—and there's no guarantee they'll get it all or that it won't return."

"So what's the point?" I ask. "Why bother?"

"It can help clean up a blockage that might be inhibiting pregnancy. And it could decrease the pain for a while."

I'm horrified by my research. Endometriosis is when uterine cells grow outside the uterus. They can bind organs together like glue, create blockages and excruciating pain. There are different surgical approaches, hormonal treatments, and pain management—but there is no cure.

I leave support groups for endometriosis sufferers just two weeks after I find them. It's discouraging to hear about multiple surgeries that offer little-to-no relief—and the constant pushing of adoption to those coping with infertility.

No matter where I go, people seem to think adoption is some magical cure. It's no wonder to me now how so many of us adoptees were set up to fail from the start.

When I tell Jae-Mee about the options, he asks, "What does your gut say?"

"I think my gut has run away crying. But my head says not to inflict any more pain on my body. My heart, though—that's another story."

"Well, you've got to do something about all this pain."

I shake my head. "The whole process seems like too much."

"If it's the money, we'll find a way."

"It's not just the money. I can't even use birth control because it upsets my whole system—and hormonal treatment is recommended for both fertility and pain management. I'm starting to think that if a baby doesn't happen on its own, then maybe I need to be okay with that. I'm just not sure if I can be."

Looking out at the bay, Jae-Mee says, "You know I'd love to have a baby with you. But I'm also pretty sure our life could still be great if it doesn't happen."

"You may think so now but there's no guarantee. You can't know how you'll feel when it's truly over. I know it's not entirely rational, but I kinda feel like I should let you go now so you can find someone who can have your baby."

Jae-Mee looks surprised and then scowls. "I find that a wee bit offensive. I'm a grown ass man. I know what I want. I'd rather be with you—with or without a baby—than be with some other woman and a supposed guaranteed child, if such thing exists."

"I know what I'm saying isn't fair to either of us. It's just something I'm afraid of. I'm used to feeling responsible for my effect on other people."

"I'm not one of those guys who grew up wanting to be a dad. It was an awesome feeling when you were pregnant with Jang-Mi, but it isn't a life goal or a deal breaker."

"What if you feel empty or incomplete when it's no longer an option?"

"Of course I can't promise that won't happen. But it's honestly not on my radar. We all eventually have disappointments in life to deal with. Right now, all I want is for you to be healthy and happy. If you think doing everything we can to make a baby will make you happiest, let's do that. If you want to try surgery for the stomach pain, I'm all for it. We'll find a way to raise the dough, either way. It's your body. Whatever you want, I'll support."

"I wish you were more decisive." I'm only half-joking.

"You wish you were more decisive."

I throw a seat cushion at him for being right.

"Everyone in the toxic parents support group talks about creating your own family," I tell him. "Like it's just that easy."

"Family can mean many things."

I groan. "Like chosen family? It's not the same thing."

"No, but it can still be rewarding. That's not what I meant anyway," he explains. "We could get a dog, maybe look into fostering someday... There are other ways to love and have an impact."

"I'd have to get over the longing to have someone in the world who's an undeniable part of me. But even facing that possible reality now is too hard. And time's running out."

"You might never need to face it at all. I still think it's too soon for all that."

"Look—I need to emotionally prepare ten steps ahead. It's what I've always done, never knowing what to expect."

IMPROBABLE BIRTHDAY

I like to take long walks by myself on my legally recognized birthday. International adoptee records are often falsified in lieu of available facts. But it's the date I've had on record for about thirty-eight years, so I figure it's as good as any.

I used to fear that thinking of the woman who bore me was a thought crime against the Stones. But disowned from the Stones, I'm free to wonder as much as I like. Ascending the Huckleberry Trail, between the wildflowers and redwoods, I allow myself to finally go there.

In glimpses resisted throughout life, my mind tried to form what she was. A rape or murder victim. A grieving woman whose infant was stolen. A prostitute. A rejected girl who found herself knocked up. But today, for the first time, I think of who she might have been—and if she's still alive, who she might be.

As my hand instinctively reaches to graze an indigo flower, I wonder if she might have reached for the same. Did she, too, wish for blue eyes as a child? Or perhaps not, being raised among Koreans.

How much did growing up in a vastly different culture and environment keep me from my true nature? Did it rob me of the patterns that may have otherwise been neatly overlaid atop hers?

Was she an artist? Did she paint or sing? She might have danced or played the Korean drums, something I witnessed when Jae-Mee's parents took us to the Seollal performance.

Did she enjoy nature as much as I do? When she breathed in the air by the sea, did it make her feel nearly anything was possible? Or did leaving or losing me take that from her?

I wonder if the features I dislike on myself are her doing or my birth father's. And then I realize it's too much to consider a birth father, given the adoptive one I had and just lost.

If I told her some truths—that I was brought into perceived wealth, had plenty to eat, decent schooling, and a few friends along the way—the unfinished picture it would paint is a lie.

And if she did send me off to a better life, I hope our paths never cross again. I can't look her in the eyes and tell her a lie or the truth. I hope she still believes in the fantasy—that I was better off without her. And, who knows? Maybe I am.

Would I have preferred to live in poverty, ostracized by our own people who pitied us, but still have my natural mother? Knowing who you are and where you come from matters so much. What would it have been like to have leaned on each other to get by? How close might we feel with that sense of entitled belonging?

Did she cry? Did she miss me? Does she think of me on the day I was born? Does she mention me in her prayers? Does she curse herself for having me gone?

Or perhaps my absence from her afforded her the life she dreamt for herself. And so buying into the promise that adoption would allow me a better life too made it feel right.

Maybe now she is happy with legitimate children and a husband who doesn't know I exist. If they're doing well, it might not be so bad to have been the sacrifice. Perhaps it would give my life more meaning.

If Jang-Mi had survived, would she resemble this woman I both long to and hesitate to call omma?

If I have children, will it inspire me to track her down? How might that go? Would it disrupt her life? Would she reject me again? Or would she tearfully open her arms wide, forcing us to learn our native tongue?

And what if someday I search and find it's too late?

If I'm fair, I suppose my denial and indifference wasn't just out of fear of upsetting the Stones. Perhaps it also shielded me. As it's impossible today to imagine my birth father, contemplating my birth mother was too overwhelming. Even now, it feels heavy—so heavy that I know I must leave the bulk of the weight on this trail. When other areas of my life are more developed, it might be time to revisit. And that will have to be good enough.

There are several ways my life could have gone. But this is the life I have. So while it's okay to wonder, this is the life I must keep choosing.

Whatever the circumstances that led to my adoption; whoever and whatever my birth mother was—today, on my possible but improbable birthday, I wish her peace.

ONE YEAR LATER

I've rekindled an old flame and it feels like falling in love.

Brushing yellow paint across canvas, what's usually disconnected feels somehow complete. It's like channeling the truth through my subconscious and allowing it to work through my body. It's both meditative and empowering.

It's hard to believe that eighteen years ago, I gave this all up for Mother. I try not to curse myself for it—or any other decisions I made against my best interest in pursuit of love. My past self has been through enough. There's no need to continue berating that girl.

Making art doesn't have me feeling self-conscious, seeking approval, or worrying that I'm not enough. I'm not pressured to create masterpieces. I take joy in being reacquainted. Painting accepts me in ways that the Stones never could. And thankfully, it's also forgiving. It rolls out the welcome mat without any demands.

Sometimes while I work on the balcony alongside Jang-Mi, Jae-Mee works on song lyrics for the band he's started. He sits in the opposite corner, strumming and humming and scribbling down words.

In ripples of awareness outside my flow, I realize my good fortune.

My stomach pain isn't gone but it's more manageable after

much trial and error. It's amazing how much brighter the world seems when you're not constantly doubled-over in pain.

We haven't yet conceived another child, and I'm working on making peace with that. Truth be told, I'm not sure I ever will. But each day, I try.

As I paint, I contemplate the art of not getting what we want. I wonder how it shapes us when we dance on the precipice of ambition and acceptance. I ruminate on the human desire to make sense of the senseless; applying meaning to things that have none. And I admire persistence but consider the damage often done when crossed with entitlement.

I forgive us all for our human fragility—so long as we hurt no one for it.

I imagine what Jae-Mee and I might experience if we remain without child. And although we might have a wonderful life, I can't believe it will be thanks to Jang-Mi's loss or a god that deemed it so. I hang onto the responsibility of truth, science, and faith in oneself.

And I don't fault anyone for having their own ways of getting through life, but this is mine. Some people need to hold onto a little more control and some need to relinquish it.

I also understand the grace in thanking those who've hurt us for giving us reason to grow. And in some ways, perhaps it delivers the knockout blow—assuming those who've hurt us still don't wish us well and wouldn't want to contribute to our success. But you'll never hear me do that. I've worked too hard for any peace I have and refuse to attribute it to my worst misfortunes.

That said, I do believe in a brand of forgiveness—one that doesn't wash things away or numb it to neutral ground, but one that eventually chooses to lessen the grip on what's hurt us. Those memories have too many thorns to hold for too long. And the narratives they recycle don't serve our future.

Sometimes I still hear the old voices and see the old footage of worse days gone. But more often as time passes, I'm able to turn them off. I've gotten all I can from them now.

Too many times, I've begged for the switch. But now I see that there is no switch. There's just a lifetime of awareness and balance. Emotional healing is not a goal or destination; it's a practice. The way I see it, you might as well fill that life with as many fulfilling people and things as possible.

Lost deep in my own inner-world, I'm jolted by Jae-Mee's voice from inside the apartment. "Hey Shay, can you help me with something when you have a sec?"

"Sure, just a minute," I call, before adding a few more yellow strokes to the canvas.

I lay the brush flat, wipe my hands on my painting skirt, and head indoors.

"Surprise!" shouts a small group of people.

I squint to adjust my eyes to the dim room. Standing before me with anticipation are Jae-Mee's three bandmates, my friend Sarah from yoga, a couple of local adoptees I've grown fond of, and someone I sharpen my eyes on for a moment, wondering if she's a local KAD who tagged along. And then I place who she is.

My knees weaken. I crouch down a little, covering my mouth with my hands as I screech, "No way!" She comes running to me and it's a whirlwind of hugs, laughter, and tears.

Shae says, "Oh my God. I've missed you so much."

"I've missed you too! I can't believe you're really here!"

I glance at Jae-Mee and ask, "How'd you do this?"

"I remembered you telling me how you found Shae again.

I had a college buddy named Mike Cooper so her dad's name stuck with me. I tracked him down and he gave me her number. And you say I don't listen. Pfft."

"Happy birthday!" shouts Sarah.

"Happy birthday!" The others follow.

Dropping into a chair, still spinning from the shock and awe, I tell them, "You know, this is the first time it's ever felt like it could be my birthday."

THE WRONG WOMAN

When I first recognize her, my heart stops. I freeze. My body involuntarily shakes. I ground myself by reciting in my head, I'm Shay Nari Song. I live in California. I'm a painter and this is my show.

Sarah from yoga's husband offered me the show last month when we had them over for dinner. He thought my work was bold and unusual for the area. I didn't feel ready, but reminded myself that oftentimes when we do, it's too late.

I'm mind-mapping her features onto the woman I last saw. Her hair's not red or blonde but a mousy brown. She wears oversized tortoiseshell glasses and comfortably-fitting clothes. She doesn't seem to have on much makeup.

Jae-Mee sidles up to me and asks, "Do you know them?"

And only then do I notice the toddler—who looks just like Mother—sitting in the stroller alongside her.

"It's Myra."

His jaw drops.

I tug at him. "Come on. Let's go get a drink."

On the short walk to the bar, a storm's throwing shrapnel around in my brain. I wonder whose god would give her a daughter and take mine.

I assume Mother sent her, but can't be sure why. Does she want me to know that no matter how far I go, they'll always find me and shake me down?

The bartender hands over two raspberry bellinis. Jae-Mee and I take them, in sync. I want to pour the whole thing down my throat but stop myself halfway. I must be clear-headed for what's to follow.

And I wonder if maybe she's seen the light? Perhaps Mother needed a new scapegoat and in my absence, it's Myra. She looks different. Maybe she's changed and seeks forgiveness for all the terrible things she's said and done.

I ask myself, will I forgive her? Should I give her that? I've already forgiven her for me. But do I need to extend it to her?

Those hard, determined footsteps lack stilettos but still set my hairs on end. They remind me of the day she waltzed into the hospital and physically attacked me, certain she was in the right.

I turn around just as she approaches, catching her off-guard. It's clear from the look on her face that she was hoping to surprise me. She unwraps a piece of winterfresh gum and slips it into her mouth.

I blurt out an emotionless, "It's you."

She studies me a moment before adding a well-paced, "Little sister. You seem to be doing alright for yourself." Her eyes shift to my right. "Jae-Mee," she says, with a contemptuous nod.

"And who's this?" I ask, dropping my eyes to the child.

Lifting her out of the stroller, she tells us, "This is Theodora—after Daddy, of course. But I know. She looks more like Mother. Too bad Mother couldn't care less about her. She's too busy praising her grandsons."

I give my most even-keeled, "Nice to meet you, Theodora." I ask Myra, "Is Graham here with you?"

"No," Myra scoffs. "He's run off with some young

model—after all I did for him. Men. No offense, Jae-Mee."

Jae-Mee shrugs and rolls his eyes.

"I like your new look," I say, unsure if I mean it, but feeling the pressure to comment.

Glancing down at herself, she laughs. "This?" She lifts up her hair to reveal it's a wig, with her platinum blonde hair underneath. "I'm incognito. Graham's little plaything is doing an event in San Fran. We're going to catch him unaware after this."

"Oh," I say, realizing Myra's unapologetic visit has nothing to do with me after all.

"I had my guy verify you were still in the area and he told me about this. Good for you."

I shake off an impulse to shrug and belittle my accomplishments as I watch her eyes, full of ennui, flit around the room from piece to piece.

"Not bad for a college dropout," she adds, no doubt hoping her words catch stray ears.

"It makes me happy," I say, forcing a smile. "So, what will you do when you catch Graham with that woman?"

"I'll make sure he lives to regret his mistakes each time he writes us a check." She bends over to place Theodora back down.

Without clearing my throat, my words come out a little wobblier than I'd hoped. "And why did you choose to stop here?"

My poor delivery is like water to her dry soil. Her posture straightens, and she lifts her chiseled face. "You're my sister," she says coolly. "I missed you."

I feel nothing from her words.

"Don't you miss me? Your brothers? And Mother?"

I finish my drink and shake my head. "No, to be honest."

"Ouch."

"I miss what I never really had."

"That's stupid," she laughs. "And that's so like you."

This time I don't laugh along with her.

Stepping forward, I crouch down and whisper to Theodora, "Run, little girl. As soon as you can." I kiss her sweet head, knowing she can't understand.

I rise, placing a hand on Myra's arm. Smiling as naturally as I can, I say, "Look, I wish you the best. But don't come looking for me again. Now, I have to go mingle. There are people I have to meet."

As I walk away, she calls to me. "What—no apologies for what you did to our family?"

Eyes are on us now when I turn to say, "I'm sorry for so much, Myra. Just not what you want me to be sorry for."

Unable to bear me walking away from her, she raises her voice. "Don't you have any compassion?"

I glance at her, knowing to keep my mouth shut. I turn away.

"You'll be sorry!" she shrieks, as I continue into the crowd. "Mark my words! One day you'll regret every stupid thing you've ever done!"

I hear a glass break but don't look back.

Sarah hands me a drink. "Who was that?"

"Just someone who thinks she knows me, but she's got the wrong woman."

There's a small crowd gathering around my painting of a bright yellow bird launching into flight. I take a deep breath, push my shoulders back and chin up, and walk towards it with pride.

ACKNOWLEDGEMENTS

First and foremost, I would like to thank my personal support system for helping me get to the point in which I was able to write and complete this book. Thank you for letting me speak at great lengths and shut down as I've needed; for encouragement without judgment or unsolicited advice; for telling your stories and empowering other survivors of covert abuse; for sharing validating articles and studies; for offering incredibly heartfelt words that make me feel awkward but teach me how to accept them; for believing me and believing in me; for making me feel worthy of love. You are my husband; my friends; my therapists; my fellow survivors of adoption, abuse, and chronic illness; acquaintances who chime in now and then to offer your hearts. Without you, I would be lost. With your support, I am found.

Deep gratitude to my fierce editors, Laura Major and Susan Major of Major Developments. I'm honored to have had you both on my team to help make this a stronger book. *KEURIUM* has undoubtedly benefited from your insight, experience, and attention to so many details.

To some of my favorite writers, humanitarians, and beacons of hope—Thomas Park Clement, Lee Herrick, and Reshma McClintock—for taking time out of your busy schedules to provide *KEURIUM* with much credibility.

To various online support groups which I've leaned on in my journey towards peace and understanding.

To those who devote countless hours towards healing, activism, education, and providing space for our voices.

To the #MeToo movement and all who support it.

To the marginalized people who help each other rise—and refuse to be held back by the system.

And to my readers—for opening your hearts and allowing me a piece of your valuable time.

ABOUT THE AUTHOR

In addition to "Keurium", JS LEE is the author of the novel, "An Ode to the Humans Who've Loved and Left Me"; author and illustrator of the children's books, "For All the Lives I've Loved and Lived" and "For All the Friends I've Found"; and her memoir, "It Wasn't Love". She has a chapter in the anthology, "The Unknown Culture Club: Korean Adoptees, Then and Now".

Navigating the nuance of race, adoption, identity, and trauma, JS LEE's work aims to provoke understanding of those in the marginalized fringe. She currently resides in the Bay Area of California with her husband and two cats.

For updates and information, visit: jessicasunlee.com.

Amazon and Goodreads reviews carry a lot of weight.
If you think this story is a worthwhile read, it would mean the
world to me if you'd so kindly review it online. It will increase
visibility, giving others a chance to discover it. Feel free to
share your favorite quotes and spread the word—while
omitting spoilers, of course.
Thank you!